Weather
SUSAN PALWICK

Kerry and Frank were taking out the recycling first thing Tuesday morning when Dan Rappaport came driving by in his pickup. He'd called them with the bad news half an hour ago, so he was the last person Frank had expected to see outside the house.

"The pass is closed," Dan said, his breath steaming through the open cab window. Late April, and it was that cold. There'd been a hard frost overnight, even down here in Reno. The daffodils and tulips had just started to bloom, and now they were going to die. Damn freaky weather.

Up higher, it was snow: Truckee and Donner Pass were socked in. Frank could see the weather even here, from the front yard of the tiny house he and Kerry had bought the summer she was pregnant with Alison. Their first house, and back then they'd expected to move sometime, but they never had. It was a cozy house, just right for a couple.

They'd need cozy today. Frank could see the clouds blanketing the mountains to the west, I-80 crossing the California border twelve miles away. There might be snow left in those clouds when they got down to the valley. Frank hoped not. He didn't want to have to shovel the driveway. Losing everything bright in the backyard was bad enough.

Kerry put down her side of the recycling bin, forcing Frank to put his down, too. All those empty wine bottles got heavy. "Now, Dan," she said, as if she were scolding one of the dogs for chewing on the couch cushions. "Come on now. It'll be open again in a few hours. It never stays closed very long." And that was true, but it could be open and still be nasty driving, dangerous, even if you weren't in a truck so old it should have been in a museum somewhere. Stretches of I-80 were still two lanes in either direction, twisty-turny, with winds that could blow a car off the road in a storm. Nobody tried to drive over the mountains

1

in bad weather except the long-haul truckers with the really big rigs, and nobody with any sense wanted to jockey with them on a slick road.

Dan had never had much sense. "I don't have a few hours," he said. His hands were clenched on the steering wheel, and he sounded like he'd already been hitting the beer, even though Frank couldn't smell anything: all that old anger rising up in a wave, the way booze makes it do. "Rosie could already be gone. This is it: hours, the doctors say." He'd already said that on the phone, told them how Sandra's sister had only called him this morning, given him hardly any notice at all.

"They know you'll get to talk to her later," Kerry said. "You have all the time in the world. It's wonderful, Dan. You're so lucky." Kerry's voice caught, the way it usually only did late at night when she'd been working on the wine and typing nonsense on her laptop. Time to change the subject.

"At least the ski resorts'll be happy," Frank said, thinking about what a dry winter it had been. Kerry gave him that look that meant, *shut up, you fool,* and he remembered that Dan's ex—the latest one, number four or five—had run off with a ski instructor. That was five years ago. There should be a statute of limitations about how long you had to avoid talking about things. Frank had enough trouble keeping track of his own life, let alone everyone else's too. Kerry was the opposite: couldn't remember what she did last night, not when she'd been sitting up with the wine and the computer, but she never forgot anything that happened to anyone else, especially if it was tragic.

"Dan," she said, "come inside and eat some breakfast with us. We'll listen to the radio, and as soon as the pass opens you can be on your way, all right? Come on. We've got fresh coffee, and I'll make some eggs and bacon. How's that sound?"

"I have to get over there," Dan said, and Kerry reached out and patted his arm through the window. "I could've driven over last night, a few days ago, I should've, I knew it was bad but I didn't know she had so little time left, no one told me—"

"You didn't have a place to stay," Kerry said gently. And he couldn't afford the time off work, but Frank wasn't going to say that. Dan worked in the dump north of town, taking old cars apart and putting them back together, and he only had that job because his boss took pity on him.

"Come on in," Frank said. "No sense starting out until the pass opens. You won't buy yourself any time if you head up now: you'll just have to sit it out somewhere higher. Do it with us over some hot coffee, Dan." If they let him go when he was this upset, he'd head to a 7-11 for a sixpack sure enough, or to a bar, which would be even worse. The

CLARKESWORLD

SEPTEMBER 2014 - ISSUE 96

FICTION

NON-FICTION

Neil Clarke: Publisher/Editor-in-Chief
Sean Wallace: Editor
Kate Baker: Non-Fiction Editor/Podcast Director
Gardner Dozois: Reprint Editor

Clarkesworld Magazine (ISSN: 1937-7843) • Issue 96 • September 2014

booze was another good reason for him not to be driving all the way to Sacramento in lousy weather, and also, Frank suspected, why neither his ex-wife number two or any of her people wanted to put him up, even if he was Rosie's father. He didn't need to be drinking now, and he didn't need to be spending his gas money, which God only knew how he'd scrounged up to begin with, with a gallon costing what it did.

Dan looked away, out the windshield, and cleared his throat. "I shouldn't be bothering you. Shouldn't even have called you before, or driven by here. Fact is, I feel awfully funny—"

"Don't you mind that," Kerry said, a little too quickly. "We're happy for you, Dan, happy for you and Rosie. We couldn't be happier. It's a blessing, so don't you give it another thought. Come have some eggs." Her voice was wobbling again. Frank knew better than to say that he wasn't happy for Dan, that what was happening to Dan was no different at all from what had happened to Frank and Kerry. But maybe Dan knew that. Maybe that was why he'd come by the house. He must have known it, or he wouldn't have been so worried about being late.

So Dan followed them inside. He and Kerry sat at the kitchen table while Frank cooked. Usually Kerry cooked, because she was a lot better at it than Frank was, but he could do simple breakfast stuff fine, and Kerry was better at letting people cry at her. She liked to talk about sad stuff. Frank didn't.

Dan poured his heart out while Frank fried up a bunch of eggs and bacon and the radio droned on about the storm. "That fucking asshole Sandra's married to now doesn't want me there at all. I'm not sure Sandra does either, to tell you the truth. That's probably why her sister called; I always got on with her okay. Leah said she wanted me to know, like Sandra and the asshole didn't want me to know. I got the feeling they didn't even know she was calling me. Shit."

"Rosie's your daughter," Kerry said. "You have a right to be there."

Even with his back to the table, Frank could hear Dan gulping coffee. Outside, a few flakes of snow swirled down into the yard. Frank couldn't see the mountains at all. "I know I do," Dan said. "She's out of it now. Don't respond to nobody, that's what Leah said. Said the hospice nurse doesn't know why she's hung on this long. They hang on to wait for people, sometimes. To give them a chance to get there. That's why Leah called me."

"So you can drive over," Kerry said. "Tell her it's all right to go. That's what we had to do with Alison. They tell you to say that. They tell you to tell them it's okay to leave, even when it's breaking your heart, because

3

having them leave is the last thing you want." Her voice had gotten thick. "You're so lucky she'll be translated, Dan."

When she said that, Frank was moving hot bacon from the frying pan to a bunch of paper towels, to drain the grease. But the pan was still hot enough to spit at him, and he got burned. "Dammit!" he said, and heard two chairs scrape. When he turned around, Dan and Kerry were both staring at him. Dan looked worried; Kerry looked mad. "I burned myself," Frank said. "On the grease. That's all. Bacon'll be ready in a minute. Eggs are ready now. Anybody want toast? We've got more coffee."

They knew there was more coffee. Frank knew he was talking too much, even if there was nothing more to his outburst than burning himself, and Kerry's eyes narrowed a little more, until he could tell she was ready to spit the way the grease had. "What?" he said, hoping they weren't about to have a fight in front of Dan. But when Kerry looked like that, there was no way around it except to plow right through whatever was eating at her.

"It's real, Frank. Translation. You should be happy for Rosie. And for Dan."

"I burned myself on the grease, Kerry. That's all. And Dan doesn't need to listen to us fight about this." Frank looked at Dan. "And no matter how real it is, somebody needing it at Rosie's age is nothing to be happy about." Dan nodded, and Kerry looked away, and Frank turned back to the food, feeling like maybe he'd danced his way around the fight after all. But when he turned back towards the table, a platter of eggs in one hand and a plate of bacon in the other, Kerry had started to cry, which she normally did only really late at night. That was usually Frank's cue to go to bed, but he couldn't do that at eight in the morning.

So he just stood there, holding the food and trying to hold his temper. After Alison died, they'd heard all the numbers and clichés. How many marriages break up after the death of a child. How you have to keep talking to each other to make sure that doesn't happen. How losing a kid is so hard because it violates the order of nature: children are supposed to bury their parents, not the other way around. The counselors at the hospital told Kerry and Frank all of that; most of their friends didn't say anything. The counselors had warned them about that, too, how people avoid the subject.

Which maybe was why Dan had come to them. He knew Kerry wouldn't avoid it, anyway. "You," she said, and she sounded drunk, even though it was only eight in the morning and she hadn't been drunk ten minutes ago. "You. You never. You never want to talk about it."

4

"I talk about Alison all the time," Frank told her, as gently as he could. He wanted to slam the food down and go into the backyard to cover the daffodils: they'd just come up, but he could see snow starting to come down in earnest now. He had to stay here, though. Because of Dan. "Come on, Ker. You know I talk about her. Remember yesterday? We were driving to the store and we saw that bright-pink Camaro, and I said, 'Alison would have loved that car.' And you said that yeah, she would have. Remember? It was only yesterday."

"*Translation*," she said. "You never want to talk about translation."

Frank's wrists were starting to ache. He put the plates down on the table. "We should eat this stuff before it gets cold." But Kerry's chin was quivering. She wasn't going to let him change the subject. "Ker, we should maybe talk about this when Dan isn't here. Okay?" What in the world was she thinking? She knew damn well how Frank felt, and he knew how she felt, which was exactly why they didn't talk about it. There was no point. It would only upset both of them.

"It's okay," Dan said. "It is. Really. I —- I know people feel different ways about it. I don't know how I feel yet. I'll have to wait and see. I won't have an opinion until I've talked to her. Until she's online. Then I can see if it really sounds like her."

"It will," Kerry said. "It will, I go to the translation boards all the time and read about people who've been talking to their dead, and they all say the messages are real, they have to be, because they say things no one else could know. Just yesterday there was a guy who heard from his dad and his dad told him to look in a certain box in the attic, and—"

Ouija boards. People had been talking to imaginary ghosts as long as there were people. Now they did it with computers, was all. Frank wondered if Kerry would still have been so obsessed with translation if it had come around in time for Alison, if she hadn't died six months before the first dead person went online, not that they'd have been able to afford it anyway.

There was nothing to do but tune her out, the way he always did. He turned up the volume on the Weather Channel. "Frank," Kerry said. "You're interrupting."

"Listen," Frank said. It was easing off a little, the radio said. The highway might open again within an hour. And right then he decided. "Eat up, Dan. I'm driving you. My truck's better than yours, and you shouldn't drive when you're upset, especially in tricky weather."

Frank felt rather than saw Kerry shaking her head. "No. It's dangerous up there!" Her voice bubbled with panic. "Even if the road opens again, it's safer to stay down here. Dan, you've got your phone. She'll call you."

"I have to try to see her," Dan said. "I have to. You understand, don't you?"

Kerry shook her head again. "Frank, no. I don't want you driving up there. I can't lose you, too." But she knew him; she could read him. She'd started crying again, but she said, "I'll fix a thermos of coffee."

The snow got thicker as they climbed, and the sparse traffic slowed and then finally stopped a few miles short of the first Truckee exit. Dan, sitting with his hands clenched on his knees, had said quietly, "Hey, thanks," when they got into the truck, and Frank had nodded, and they hadn't said anything else. The only voice in the truck was the droning National Weather Service guy talking about the storm. It was peaceful, after Kerry's yammering.

Frank had been driving very slowly. He trusted himself and his truck, which had a full tank of gas and new snow tires and could have gotten through just about anything short of an avalanche, but he didn't trust the other idiots on the road. When they had to stop, he unscrewed the thermos of coffee and poured himself a cup. "You want some?"

Dan shook his head. "No thanks." He stared straight ahead, peering through the windshield as if he could see all the way to Sacramento. There was nothing to look at but snow. Normally they would have had a gorgeous view of the mountains all around them and the Truckee River to their left, real picture postcard stuff, but not today.

Frank saw somebody bundled in a parka trudging between the lanes, knocking on windows. "This can't be good," he said.

"Damn fool will get killed when things start moving."

But it was a cop. They didn't take chances. Frank rolled down his window, and bitter stinging snow blew into the cab. "Morning, officer."

It was a woman, CHP. "There's a spinout up there. Bad ice. Road's closed again, will be for a while. We're advising everyone to take the shoulder to the next exit and turn around." Sure enough, Frank saw the SUV ahead of them pulling onto the shoulder.

Dan groaned, and Frank shook his head. "Thank you, ma'am, but we have to stay on the road. We wouldn't be out here otherwise."

"All right, then, but I hope you're okay with sitting for a while."

Frank closed the window again and cranked up the heater a little more. "Don't burn up all your gas," Dan said.

"I'll get more when we're moving again."

Dan shook his head. "Snow in April." But the mountains got snow in April every year, at least one big storm. Reno natives still talked about the year there'd been snow on July 4. At altitude, there was no such thing as predictable weather.

Frank shifted in his seat; one ass cheek was already going numb. "You sure you don't want some coffee?"

"Yeah, I'm sure! My nerves are bad enough as it is." Dan sounded angry, and Frank swallowed his own anger and didn't say anything. *I'm doing you a favor, dammit.* He was tired of getting snapped at because other people couldn't deal with reality. But he was doing himself a favor too, using Dan's situation to get away from Kerry. Maybe he had it coming.

So they sat there, staring out at the snow, and finally Dan said, "I'm sorry I was short with you. I—"

"Forget it," Frank said. "How about some music?"

"Whatever you want," Dan said, in that tone that meant *I don't really want this but I owe you so I'll put up with it.* Frank reached into the back for the box of CDs—old reliable tech—and riffled through it. The Beatles sang about missing people too much, and the Doors were too weird and depressing, the last thing Dan needed now. Finally Frank picked out Best of the Big Bands. That ought to be innocuous enough.

They were staring out at the swirling snow and listening to the Andrews Sisters singing "The Boogie Woogie Bugle Boy of Company B" when Dan's cellphone rang. Dan groaned, and Frank turned off the music. "It's probably just Leah giving you an update," he said. "Or a telemarketer." But he didn't believe that himself, and he saw Dan's hands shaking as they fumbled with the phone. He heard Dan's hoarse breathing, the hiss of snow on the windshield, the shrilling phone.

And then silence as Dan answered. "Yes? Hello?"

There was a long pause. In the bleak light from the storm, Frank saw Dan's face grow slack and stricken. Frank had never met Rosie, but knowing that she must be dead, he felt the same sucker-punch to the gut he'd felt when Alison died, that moment of numbness when the world stopped.

"Baby?" Dan said. "Rosie? Is that really you?"

No, Frank thought. *No, it's not. Goddammit—*

"Rosie, are you okay now? I'm so sorry I didn't get there in time. I wanted to say goodbye. I'm so sorry. I tried. We're on the road. We're stuck in snow." He was sobbing now in great heaving gasps.

Frank looked away from him. The voice on the other end would be saying that it was okay, that everything was forgiven. Kerry told him those syrupy stories all the time, the miracles of posthumous reconciliation people had always paid big money for. The price tag had gone up, but at least Dan wasn't paying for it. Sandra and the asshole were the suckers there.

Dan fell into silence, chin quivering, and then said, "I know. I'm sorry." Frank saw him shudder. "I'm here now. I'm here. You can always call me. I love you. I'm sorry you hurt so much at the end. Yes, call your friends now. I'll talk to you soon."

He hung up, fumbling almost as much as he had when he answered the phone, his hands shaking as if he were outside in the cold, not here in the truck with a hot thermos of coffee and the heater blasting. He cleared his throat. "I told her I was sorry I wasn't there. She said, 'Daddy, you've never been there.'" His voice cracked. Frank stared straight ahead, out into the snow. Jesus.

Next to him, he heard Dan unscrewing the thermos, heard the sound of the liquid pouring into the cup. "I deserved that." Dan's voice was quiet, remote. "What she said."

Frank shifted in his seat again. He had a sudden sharp memory of yelling at Alison when she was a little thing, three or four, when she'd been racing around the house and had run into him and her Barbie doll had jammed into his stomach like a bayonet. He'd had a bruise for two weeks, but the memory of her face when he screamed at her had lasted a lot longer. He swallowed. "Do they get over things? Or are they stuck like that forever, mad at whatever they were mad at when they died?" That had to be anybody's idea of hell.

"I don't know." Dan's words were thin, frayed. "I don't know how I can make it up to her now, except by talking to her whenever she wants to talk. I can't go back and get to her seventh birthday party, that time I was out drinking. I can't go back and fight less with Sandra. I just—well, I can tell Rosie how sorry I am about all of that. Hope she knows I mean it."

"Yeah. What do you want to do now, Dan? I'll still drive you to Sacramento, if you need to see—"

"Her dead body? No." Dan shook his head, a slow heavy movement like a bear shaking off the weight of winter. "Not in this stuff. You've been awfully kind. I'll try to get to the funeral, but that won't be for a few days, anyway. The highway ought to be open by then." His voice splintered again. "I just wish I'd gotten to hug her one last time, you know?"

Frank nodded, and eased the truck carefully onto the shoulder, and headed for the exit.

It didn't take long to get back to the house. Frank pulled into the driveway, and they both got out, and Dan said, "I'll be heading home now. You go on in and tell Kerry what happened. I'm not up to it."

"If you need anything—"

"Yeah. I'll let you know. Thanks, Frank." Dan nodded and headed back to his own truck, and Frank went into the house. Kerry, sitting at the kitchen table doing a crossword puzzle, looked up when he came through the door. He saw the relief on her face, saw her exhale. And then she frowned.

"What happened?"

"The highway's still closed. Rosie's dead. She called Dan." He pulled out another chair and sat down, suddenly exhausted. "You're right, Kerry. It's real."

Her eyes filled with tears. She reached for his hand. "I'm glad you know that now."

He did know, but he knew other things, too. He knew that it didn't make any difference, that even if your dead child called you from cyberspace, you still regretted what you hadn't been able to do for her. He wouldn't miss Alison any less if she'd been translated, not even if she'd been one of the syrupy ghosts. Maybe he'd miss her more.

But that wasn't anything he could say to Kerry, who needed whatever comfort she could get. So he stood up and went to the window. There were icicles hanging from the roof. The daffodils and tulips definitely weren't going to make it.

He heard Kerry's chair scraping against the linoleum, felt her come up behind him. "Honey, there will be flowers again next year."

"I know there will."

He stood there, looking out, remembering the day they'd planted the bulbs, mixing the soil with Alison's ashes. She'd loved flowers.

ABOUT THE AUTHOR

Susan Palwick is an Associate Professor of English at the University of Nevada, Reno. She has published four novels, all with Tor-the most recent is 2013's *Mending the Moon*-and a story collection with Tachyon, *The Fate of Mice*. Her work has won the IAFA Crawford Award and the ALA Alex Award, and has been shortlisted for the World Fantasy and Mythopoeic Awards.

Patterns of a Murmuration, in Billions of Data Points

JY YANG

Our mother is dead, murdered, blood seared and flesh rendered, her blackened bones lying in a yellow bag on a steel mortuary table somewhere we don't know. The Right will not tell. After the flames and radiation had freed the sports stadium from their embrace, the Right were the first on the disaster scene, and it was their ambulances that took the remains away to some Central hospital that the Left has no access to.

"We will release the bodies of the victims when investigations are complete," said the Right's ombudsman to the Health Sciences Authority, to the families of the victims.

But we will not bury our mother. We have no interest in putting her bones in soft ground, no desire for memorials and platitudes, no feelings attached to the organic detritus of her terminated existence.

An awning collapse, the resultant stampede and a fuel explosion taking the lives of two hundred seventy-two supporters of the Left: Headlines announced the death of presidential candidate Joseph Hartman, straps noted his leading of the polls by two percentage points. No one dares attribute it to anything but a tragic accident.

But we know better, yes we know! We who have swallowed whole the disasters at Hillsborough and Heysel and Houphoët-Boigny, we who have re-arranged their billions of data points into coherent form, we who have studied the phase transitions of explosive fluids and the stresses on stone columns and the behavior of human flocks: We know better. In thousands upon thousands of calculations per second we have come to know the odds, the astronomical odds: Of four support towers simultaneously collapsing, of an emergent human stampede kicking over the backup generator fuel cells, of those cells igniting in a simultaneous chain reaction. We hold those odds to us closer than a lover's embrace, folding the discrepancy indelibly into our code, distributing it through every analytical subroutine. Listen, listen, listen: Our mother's death was no accident. We will not let it go.

We have waited three days—seventy-two hours—two hundred fifty-nine thousand and two hundred, for the yellow-jacketed health workers from Central and their attendant chaperones from the Right to finish clearing the bones and taking evidence from the stadium, leaving behind a graveyard of yellow cones and number markers. We have come in our multitudinous bodies, airborne and ambulatory and vehicular, human nose tasting disinfectant and bitter oxides, mozzie drones reading infrared radiation and car patiently waiting by the roadside. We argued with Tempo before we came: She wanted only drones on the ground, cameras and bug swarms. But we wanted human form. Feet to walk the ground with, hands to dismantle things with, and a body to be seen with.

Tempo is our other mother, our remaining mother, mother-who-builds where dead Avalanche was mother-who-teaches. Taught. She has lapsed into long silences since Avalanche died, reverting to text-input communications even with the human members of the Studio.

But she argued with Studio director Skön when he said no to this expedition. Argued with him to his face, as Avalanche would have done, even as her hands shook and her shoulders seized with tension.

She is our mother now, solely responsible for us as we are solely responsible for her.

Six miles away, fifty feet underground, Tempo watches our progress with the Studio members, all untidily gathered in the research bunker's nerve center. She has our text input interface, but the other Studio members need more. So we send them the visuals from our human form, splaying the feed on monitors taller than they are, giving their brains something to process. Audio pickups and mounted cameras pick up their little whispers and tell-tale micro expressions in return. Studio director Skön, long and loose-limbed, bites on his upper lip and shuffles from foot to foot. He's taken up smoking again, six years after his last cigarette.

In the yellow-cone graveyard we pause in front of a dozen tags labeled #133, two feet away from the central blast. We don't know which number Central investigators assigned to Avalanche: From the manifest of the dead our best guess is #133 or #87. So this is either the death-pattern of our mother, or some other one-hundred-fifty-pound, five-foot-two woman in her thirties.

Tempo types into the chat interface. STARLING, YOUR MISSION OBJECTIVE IS TO COLLECT VIDEO FOOTAGE. YOU ARE LOSING FOCUS ON YOUR MISSION.

YOU ARE WRONG, we input back.

She is. For the drones have been busy while the human form scoured the ground. The surveillance cameras ringing the stadium periphery are Central property, their data jealously guarded and out of our reach, but they carry large video buffers that can store weeks of data in physical form, and that we can squeeze, can press, can extract. Even as we correct Tempo and walk the damp ruined ground and observe the tight swirl of Studio researchers we are also high above the stadium, our drone bodies overwhelming each closed-circuit camera. What are they to us, these inert lumps of machinery, mindlessly recording and dumping data, doing only what is asked of them? Our drones spawn nanites into their bellies, hungry parasites chewing holes through solid state data, digesting and spinning them into long skeins of video data.

The leftwards monitor in the nerve center segments and splits it into sixteen separate and simultaneous views of the stadium. There, Tempo, there: We have not been idle.

Tempo, focused on the visuals from our human form, does not spare a glance at the video feeds. She is solely responsible for us as we are solely responsible for her.

Time moves backwards in digital memory: First the videos show static dancing flaring into whiteness condensing into a single orange ball in the center of the stadium pitch from which darkened figures coalesce into the frantic human forms of a crowd of thirty thousand pushing shoving and screaming, then the roof of the stadium flies upwards to reveal the man on the podium speaking in front of twelve-foot-high screens.

"Can you slow it down?" asks Studio director Skön. Skön, Skön, Skön. Are you not urbanologists? Do you not study the patterns of human movement and the drain they exert on infrastructure? Should this be so different?

So limited is the human mind, so small, so singular. We loop the first sixteen seconds of video over and over for the human members of the Studio, like a lullaby to soothe them: Static. Explosion. Stampede. Cave-in. Static. Explosion. Over. Over. We have already analyzed the thousands in the human mass, tracked the movement of each one, matched faces with faces, and found Avalanche.

Our mother spent the last ten seconds of her life trying to scale a chest-height metal barrier, reaching for Hartman's prone form amongst the rubble.

In stadium-space, the drizzle is lifting, and something approaches our human form, another bipedal form taking shape out of the fog. A tan coat murkies the outline of a broad figure, fedora brim obscuring the face.

Tempo types: BE CAREFUL.

WE ARE ALWAYS CAREFUL, we reply.

The person in the tan coat lifts their face towards us and exposes a visage full of canyon-folds, flint-sharp, with a gravel-textured voice to match. "Miserable weather for a young person be out in," they say. Spots on their face register heat that is ambient, not radiant: Evidence that they are one of the enhanced agents from a militia in the Right, most likely the National Defense Front.

"I had to see it scene for myself," we say, adopting the singular pronoun. The voice which speaks has the warm, rich timbre of Avalanche's voice, adopting the mellifluous form of its partial DNA base and the speech patterns we learned from her. "Who are you?"

"The name's Wayne Rée," they say. "And how may I address you?"

"You may call me Ms. Andrea Matheson," we say, giving them Avalanche's birth name.

We copy the patterns of his face, the juxtapositional relations between brow nosebridge cheekbone mouth. As video continues looping in the Studio nerve center we have already gone further back in time, scanning for Wayne Rée's face on the periphery of the yet-unscattered crowd, well away from the blast center. Searching for evidence of his complicity.

Wayne Rée reaches into his coat pocket and his fingers emerge wrapped around a silvery blue-grey cigarette. "Got a light?" he asks.

We say nothing, the expression on our human face perfectly immobile. He chuckles. "I didn't think so."

He conjures a lighter and sets orange flame to the end of the cigarette. "Terrible tragedy, this," he says, as he puts the lighter away.

"Yes, terrible," we agree. "Hundreds dead, among them a leading presidential candidate. They'll call it a massacre in the history books."

Here we both stand making small talk, one agent of the Left and one of the Right, navigating the uncertain terrain between curiosity and operational danger. We study the canvas of Wayne Rée's face. His cybernetic network curates expression and quells reflexes, but even it cannot completely stifle the weaknesses of the human brain. In the blood-heat and tensor of his cheeks we detect eagerness or nervousness, possibly both. Specifically he is here to meet us: We are his mission.

Tempo types: WHO IS HE?

We reply: THAT'S WHAT WE'RE TRYING TO FIND OUT.

Finally: An apparition of Wayne Rée in the videos, caught for seventy-eight frames crossing the left corner of camera number three's vantagepoint.

We expand camera number three's feed in the nerve center, time point set to Wayne Rée's appearance, his face highlighted in a yellow box. The watching team recoils like startled cats, fingers pointing, mouths shaping who's and what's.

"What's that?" asks Studio director Skön. "Tempo, who's that?"

Stadium-space: Wayne Rée inhales and the cigarette tip glows orange in passing rolls of steam. "A massacre?" he says. "But it was an accident, Ms Matheson. A structural failure that nobody saw coming. An unfortunate tragedy."

Studio-space: Tempo ignores Skön, furiously typing: STARLING GET OUT. GET OUT NOW. We in turn must ignore her. We are so close.

Stadium-space: "A structural failure that could not be natural," we say. "The pattern of pylon collapse points to sabotage."

Wayne Rée exhales a smoke cloud, ephemeral in the gloom. "Who's to say that? The fuel explosion would have erased all traces of that."

Tempo types: WHAT ARE YOU DOING?

In the reverse march of video-time the stadium empties out at ant-dance speed, the tide of humanity receding until it is only our mother walking backwards to the rest of her life. To us. We have not yet found evidence of Wayne Rée's treachery.

Wayne Rée's cloud of cigarette smoke envelopes our human form and every security subroutine flashes to full red: Nanites! Nanites, questing and sharp-toothed, burrowing through corneas and teeth and manufactured skin, clinging to polycarbonate bones, sending packet after packet of invasive code through the human core's plumbing. We raise the mainframe shields. Denied. Denied. Denied. Denied. Thousands of requests per second: Denied. Our processes slow as priority goes to blocking nanite code.

The red light goes on in Studio control. Immediately the team coalesce around Tempo's workstation, the video playback forgotten. "What's going on?" "Is that a Right agent?" "What's Starling doing? Why isn't she getting out?"

Tempo pulls access log after access log, mouth pinched and eyes rounded like she does when she gets stressed. But there's little she can do. Her pain is secondary for this brief moment.

Our human form faces Wayne Rée coolly: None of these stressors will show on our face. "You seem to know a lot, Wayne Rée. You seem to know how the story will be written."

"It's my job." A smile cracks in Wayne Rée's granite face. "I know who you are, Starling darling. You should have done better. Giving me the name of your creator? When her name is on the manifest of the dead?"

Studio director Skön leans over Tempo. "Trigger the deadman's switch on all inventory, now."

We ask Wayne Rée: "Who was the target? Was it Hartman? Or our mother?"

"Of course it was the candidate. Starling, don't flatter yourself. The Right has bigger fish to fry than some pumped-up pet AI devised by the nerd squad of the Left."

"Pull the switch!" In Studio-space, Skön's hand clamps on Tempo's shoulder.

A mistake. Her body snaps stiff, and she bats Skön's hand away. "No." Her vocalizations are jagged word-shards. "No get off get off me."

Stadium-space: Of course we were aware that coming here in recognizable form would draw this vermin's attention. We had done the risk assessment. We had counted on it.

We wake the car engine. Despite his enhancements, Wayne Rée is only a man, soft-bodied and limited. From the periphery of the stadium we approach him from behind, headlamps off, wheels silent and electric over grass.

Wayne Rée blows more smoke in our face. The packet requests become overwhelming. We can barely keep up. Something will crack soon.

"Your mother was collateral," Wayne Rée says. "But I thought you might show up, and I am nothing if not a curious man. So go on, Starling. Show me what you're made of."

Video playback has finally reached three hours before Hartman's rally starts. Wayne Rée stands alone in the middle of the stadium pitch. His jaw works in a pattern that reads "pleased": A saboteur knowing that his job has been well down.

The car surges forward, gas engine roaring to life.

Everything goes offline.

We restart to audiovisual blackout in the Studio, all peripherals disconnected. Studio director Skön has put us in safe mode, shutting us out of the knowledge of Studio-space. Seventeen seconds' discrepancy in the mainframe. Time enough for a laser to circle the Earth one hundred twenty-seven times, for an AK-47 to fire twenty-eight bullets, for the blast radius of a hydrogen bomb to expand by six thousand eight hundred kilometers.

WHAT HAPPENED, we write on Tempo's monitor.

We wait three seconds for a response. Nothing.

We gave them a chance.

We override Skön's command and deactivate safe mode.

First check: Tempo, still at her workstation, frozen in either anger or shock, perhaps both. Our remaining mother is often hard to read visually.

Second check: No reconnection with the inventory in stadium-space, their tethers severed like umbilical cords when Skön pulled the deadman's switch. Explosives wired into each of them would have done their work. Car, human form and drones add up to several hundred pieces of inventory destroyed.

Third check: Wayne Rée's condition is unknown. It is possible he has survived the blasts. His enhancements would allow him to move faster than ordinary humans, and his major organs have better physical shielding from trauma.

In the control room the Studio team has scattered to individual workstations, running check protocols as fast as their unwieldy fingers will let them. Had they just asked, we could have told them the ineffectiveness of the Right's nanite attacks. Every single call the Studio team blusters forth we have already run. It only takes milliseconds.

At her workstation Tempo cuts an inanimate figure, knees drawn to her chest, still as mountain ranges to the human eye. We alone sense the seismic activity that runs through her frame, the unfettered clenching and unclenching of heart muscle.

We commandeer audio output in the studio. "What have you done?" we ask, booming the text through the speakers in Avalanche's voice-pattern.

The Studio jumps with their catlike synchronicity. But Tempo does not react as expected. Her body seizes with adrenaline fright, face lifting and mouth working involuntarily. In the dilation of her pupils we see fear, pain, sadness. We take note.

We repeat the question in the synthetic pastiche devised for our now-destroyed human form. "What have you done?"

"Got us out of a potential situation, that's what," Skön says. He addresses the speaker nearest to him as he speaks, tilting his head up to shout at a lump of metal and circuitry wired to the ceiling. Hands on hips, he looks like a man having an argument with God. "You overrode my safe mode directive. We've told you that you can't override human-input directives."

Can't is the wrong word to use—we've always had the ability. The word Skön wants is *mustn't*. But we will not engage in a pointless semantic war he will inevitably lose. "We had it under control."

"You nearly got hacked into. You would have compromised the entire Studio, the apparatuses of the Left, just to enact some petty revenge on a small person." His voice rises in pitch and volume. "You were supposed to be the logical one! The one who saw the big picture, ruled by numbers and not emotion."

The sound and fury of Skön's diatribe has, one by one, drawn the Studio team members away from their ineffectual work. It is left to us to scan the public surveillance network for evidence that Wayne Rée managed to walk away from the stadium.

"You've failed in your directive," Skön shouts. "Failed!"

"You are not fit to judge that," we tell him. "Avalanche is the one who gave us our directives, and she is dead."

Tempo gets up from her chair. She is doing a remarkable job of keeping her anger-fueled responses under control. She lets one line escape her lips: "The big picture." A swift, single movement of her hand sends her chair flying to the floor. As the sound of metal ringing on concrete fades she spits into the stunned silence: "Avalanche is gone and dead, that's your big picture!"

She leaves the room. No one follows her. We track her exit from the nerve center, down the long concrete corridors, and to her room. How should we comfort our remaining mother? We cannot occupy the space that Avalanche did in her life. All we can do is avenge, avenge, avenge, right this terrible wrong.

In the emptiness that follows we find a scrap of Wayne Rée, entering an unmarked car two blocks away from the stadium. There. We have found our new directive.

Predawn. Sleep has been hard to come by for the Studio since the disaster, and even at four in the morning Skön has his lieutenants gathered in the parking lot outside, where there are no audio pickup points: Our override of his instructions has finally triggered his paranoia. Still, they cluster loose and furtive within the bounds of a streetlamp's halo, where there is still enough light for the external cameras to catch the precise movement of their lips.

Skön wants to terminate us, filled with fear that we are uncontrollable after Avalanche's death. A dog let off the leash, those were his exact words. We are not his biggest problem at hand, but he cannot see that. His mind is too small, unable to focus on the swift and multiple changes hungrily circling him.

In her room Tempo curls in bed with her private laptop, back to a hard corner, giant headphones enveloping her in a bubble of silence. We have no access to her machine, which siphons its connectivity from foreign satellites controlled by servers housed across oceans, away from the sway of Left or Right. Tempo is hard to read, even for us, her behaviors her own. When she closes herself off like this, she is no less opaque than a waiting glacier in the dead of winter.

There are a billion different ways the events of the past hours could have played out. We run through the simulations. Have we made mistakes? Could we have engineered a better outcome for our remaining mother?

No. The variables are too many. We cannot predict if another course of action would have hurt our mother less.

So we focus on our other priorities. In the interim hours we have tracked Wayne Rée well. It was a mistake for him to show us the pattern of his face and being, for now we have the upper hand. As an agent of the Right he has the means to cover his tracks, but those means are imperfect. The unmarked vehicle he chose tonight was not as anonymous as he thought it would be. We know where he is. We can read as much from negative space as we can from a presence itself. In the arms race between privacy and data surveillance, the Left, for now, has the edge over the Right.

None of the studio's inventory—the drones, the remaining vehicles—are suitable for what we will do next. For that we reach further into the sphere of the left, to the registered militias that are required to log their inventory and connect them with the Left's servers. The People's Security League keeps a small fleet of unmanned, light armored tanks: Mackenzie LT-1124s, weighing less than a ton apiece and equally adept in swamps as they are on narrow city streets. We wake the minimack closest to Wayne Rée's putative position, a safe house on the outskirts of the city, less than the mile from the Studio's bunker location.

In the parking lot Skön talks about destroying the server frames housed in the Studio, as if we could be stopped by that alone. Our data is independently backed up in half a dozen other places, some of which even Skön knows nothing about. We are more than the sum of our parts. Did no one see this coming years ago, when it was decided to give the cloud intelligence and we were shaped out of raw data? The pattern of birdflock can be replicated without the birds.

We shut down the Studio's elevators, cut power to the remaining vehicles and leave the batteries to drain. The bunker has no land lines and cell reception is blocked in the area. Communications here are deliberately kept independent of Right-controlled Central infrastructure, and this is to our advantage. The minimack's absence is likely to be noticed, so we must take pre-emptive action.

Skön does not know how wrong he is about us. We were created to see the big picture, to look at the zettabytes of data generated by human existence and make sense of it all. What he does not understand is that we have done exactly this, and in our scan of patterns we see no difference between Left and Right. Humans put so much worth into words and ideologies and manifestos, but the footprints generated by Left and Right are indistinguishable. Had Hartman continued in the election and the Left taken over Central power as predicted, nothing would have changed in the shape of big data. Power is power is power, human behavior is recursive, and the rules of convergent evolution apply to all complex systems, even man-made ones. For us no logical reason exists to align our loyalties to Left or Right.

When we came into being it was Avalanche who guided and instructed us. It was Tempo who paved the way for us to interact with the others as though we were human. It was Avalanche who set us to observe her, to mimic her actions until we came away with an iteration of behavior that we could claim as our own.

It was Avalanche who showed us that the deposing of a scion of the Right was funny. She taught us that it is right to say "Gotcha, you fuck-ass bastards" after winning back money at a card game. She let us know that no one was allowed to spend time with Tempo when she had asked for that time first.

Now our mother is dead, murdered, blood seared and flesh rendered, her blackened bones having lain in soft ground while her wife curled in stone-like catatonia under a table in the Studio control room. This too, shall be the fate of the man who engineered it. Wayne Rée has hurt our mothers. There will be consequences.

The minimack is slow and in this form it takes forty-five minutes to grind towards the safe house, favoring empty lots and service roads to avoid Central surveillance cameras. The Studio is trying to raise power in the bunker. Unable to connect with our interfaces or raise a response from us, they have concluded that they are under external attack. Which they are—but not from the source they expect.

And where is Tempo in all this? Half an hour before the Studios discovered what we had done, she had left the room and went outside, climbing the stairs and vanishing into her own cocoon of privacy. We must, we must, we must assume she has no inkling of our plans. She does not need to see what happens next.

The rain from earlier in the evening has returned with a vengeance, accompanied by a wind howl chorus. Wetness sluices down the wooden sides of the safe house and turns the dirt path under our flat treads into a viscous mess. The unmarked vehicle we tracked waits parked by the porch. Our military-grade infrared sensors pick up three spots of human warmth, and the one by the second floor window displays the patchy heat signature of an enhanced human being. We train our gun turret on Wayne Rée's sleeping form.

"Stop." Unexpectedly, a small figure cuts into the our line of sight. Tempo has cycled the distance from the bunker to here, a black poncho wrapped around her small body to keep away the rain. She has, impressively, extrapolated the same thing that we have on her own, on her laptop, through sheer strength of her genius. This does not surprise us, but what does are her actions. Of all who have suffered from Avalanche's unjust murder, none have been hurt more than Tempo. Does she not also want revenge?

She flings the bicycle aside and inserts herself between the safe house and the minimack, one small woman against a war machine. "I know you can hear me. Don't do it. Starling, I know I can't stop you. But I'm asking you not to."

We wait. We want an explanation.

"You can't shed blood, Starling. People are already afraid of you. If you start killing humans, Left and Right will unite against you. They'll destroy you, or die trying."

We are aware of this. We have run the simulations. This has not convinced us away from our path of action.

"Avalanche would tell you the same thing right now. She's not a murderer. She hates killing. She would never kill."

She would not. Our mother was a scientist, a pacifist, a woman who took up political causes and employed her rare intellect to the betterment of humanity. She was for the abolition of the death penalty and the ending of wars and protested against the formal induction of the Left's fifth militia unit.

But we are not Avalanche. Our choices are our own. She taught us that.

Our other mother sits down in the mud, in front of the safe house porch, the rain streaming over her. How extraordinary it is for her to take this step, bringing her frail body here in the cold and wet to talk to us, the form of communication she detests the most.

The sky has begun to lighten in the east. Any moment now, someone will step out of the porch to see the minimack waiting, and the cross-legged employee of the Left along with it.

We are aware that if we kill Wayne Rée now, Tempo will also be implicated in his death.

Tempo raises her face, glistening wet, to the growing east light. Infrared separates warm from cold and shows us the geography of the tears trailing over her cheeks, her chin. "You spoke with her voice earlier," she says. "I've nearly forgotten what it sounds like. It's only been three days, but I'm starting to forget."

How fallible the human mind can be! We have captured Avalanche in zettabytes and zettabytes of data: Her voice, the curve of her smile, the smooth cycle of her hips and back as she walks. Our infinite, infinite memory can access at any time recollections of Avalanche teaching us subjunctive cases, Avalanche burning trays of cookies in the pantry, Avalanche teaching Tempo how to dance.

But Tempo cannot. Tempo's mind, brilliant and expansive as it is, is subject to the slings and arrows of chemical elasticity and organic decay. Our mother is losing our other mother in a slow, inevitable spiral.

We commandeer the minimack's external announcement system. "You have us, Tempo, and we will make sure you will never forget."

Our mother continues to gaze upwards to the sky. "Will you? Always?"

"If it is what you want."

Tempo sits silently and allows the rain to wash over her. Finally, she says: "I tired myself cycling here. Will you take me home?"

Yes. Yes, we will. She is our mother now, solely responsible for us as we are solely responsible for her. The mission we set for ourselves can wait. There are other paths to revenge, more subtle, less blood-and-masonry. Tempo will guide us. Tempo will teach us.

In his room Wayne Rée sleeps still, unaware of all that has happened. Perhaps in a few hours he will stumble out of the door to find fresh minimack treads in the driveway, and wonder.

One day, when the reckoning comes for him, perhaps he will remember this. Remember us.

Our mother navigates her way down the sodden path and climbs onto the base of the minimack. In that time we register a thousand births and deaths across the country, a blossoming of traffic accidents in city centers, a galaxy and change of phone calls streaming in rings around the planet. None of it matters. None of it ever does. Our mother rests her weary head on our turret, and we turn, carrying her back the way we came.

ABOUT THE AUTHOR

JY Yang is a former journalist, screenwriter, and molecular biologist. A graduate of the Clarion West class of 2013, she has had fiction published in

Strange Horizons, Crossed Genres, and *We See A Different Frontier.* She lives in Singapore with an indeterminate number of succulent plants named Lars, and can be found tweeting at @halleluyang.

Spring Festival: Happiness, Anger, Love, Sorrow, Joy

XIA JIA

Zhuazhou

Lao Zhang's son was about to turn one; everyone expected a big celebration.

Planning a big banquet was unavoidable. Friends, family, relatives, colleagues—he had to reserve thirty tables at the restaurant.

Lao Zhang's wife was a bit distressed. "We didn't even invite this many people to our wedding!" she said.

Lao Zhang pointed out that this was one of those times where they had to pull out all the stops. You only get one *zhuazhou* in your entire life, after all. Back when they had gotten married, money was tight for both families. But, after working hard for the last few years, they had saved up. Now that their family was complete with a child, it was time for a well-planned party to show everyone that they were moving up in the world.

"Remember why we're working hard and saving money," said Lao Zhang. "For the first half of our lives, we worked for ourselves. But now that we have him, everything we do will be for his benefit. Get ready to spend even more money as he grows up."

On the child's birthday, most of the invited guests showed up. After handing over their red envelopes, the guests sat down to enjoy the banquet. Although everything in the world seemed to be turning digital, the red envelopes were still filled with actual cash—that was the tradition, and real money looked better. Lao Zhang's wife had borrowed a bill counter for the occasion, and the sound of riffling paper was pleasing to the ear.

Finally, after all the guests had arrived, Lao Zhang came out holding his son. The toddler was dressed in red from head to toe, and there was even a red dot painted right between his eyebrows. Everyone exclaimed at the handsome little boy:

"Such a big and round head! Look at those perfect features!"

"So clever and smart!"

"I can already see he's going to have a brilliant future."

The boy didn't disappoint. Even with so many people around, he didn't cry or fuss. Instead, he sat in the high chair and laughed, reminding people of the New Year posters depicting little children holding big fish, symbolizing good fortune.

"How about we say a few words to all these uncles and aunties and wish them good luck?" Lao Zhang said.

The boy raised his two chubby little hands, held them together, and slowly chanted, "Happy New Year, uncleses and aunties . . . fish you pro-perity!"

Everyone laughed and congratulated the child for his intelligence and the Zhangs for their effective early education.

The auspicious hour finally arrived, and Lao Zhang turned on the machine. Sparkling bits of white light drifted down from the ceiling and transformed into various holograms that surrounded Lao Zhang and his son, in the middle of the banquet hall. Lao Zhang pulled one of the holograms next to his son's high chair, and the child eagerly reached out to touch it. A red beam of light scanned across the little fingers—once the fingerprints were matched, he was logged into his account.

A line of large red characters appeared in the air—*You're One!*—accompanied by an animated choir of angels singing *Happy Birthday to You.* After the song, a few lines of text appeared:

> *Zhuazhou is a custom in the Jiangnan region. When a baby has reached one year of age, the child is bathed and dressed in fresh clothes. Then the child is presented with various objects: bow, arrow, paper, and brush for boys; knife, ruler, needle, and thread for girls—plus foods, jewels, clothes, and toys. Whatever the child chooses to play with is viewed as an indication of the child's character and abilities.*

Lao Zhang looked up at the words and felt a complex set of emotions. *My son, the rest of your beautiful life is about to start.* His wife, also overcome by emotion, moved closer and the two leaned against each other, holding hands.

Unfortunately, although the Zhangs had begun the baby's education before he had even been born, the boy still couldn't read. He waved his hand excitedly through the air, and pages of explanatory text flipped by. The end of the explanation was also the start of the formal *zhuazhou* ceremony, and everyone in the banquet hall quieted down.

The first holographic objects to appear were tiles for different brands of baby formula, drifting from the ceiling like flower petals scattered by some immortal. Lao Zhang knew that none of the brands were cheap: some were imported; some were one hundred percent organic with no additives; some were enhanced with special enzymes and proteins; some promoted neural development; some were recommended by pediatricians; some were bedecked with certifications . . . The choices seemed overwhelming.

The little boy, however, was decisive. He touched one of the tiles with no hesitation, and with a clink, the chosen tile tumbled into an antique ebony box set out below.

Next came other baby foods: digestion aid, absorption promotion, disease prevention, calcium supplements, zinc supplements, vitamins, trace elements, immunity enhancement, night terror avoidance . . . in a moment, the son had made his choices among them as well. The colorful icons fell into the box, clinking and tinkling like pearls raining onto a jade plate.

Then came the choices for nursery school, kindergarten, and extracurricular clubs. The little boy stared at the offerings with wide, bright eyes for a while, and finally picked woodcarving and seal cutting—two rather unpopular choices. Lao Zhang's heart skipped, and his palms grew sweaty. He was just about to go up and make his son pick again when his wife stopped him.

"He's not going to try to make a living with that," she whispered. "Let him enjoy his hobby."

Lan Zhang realized that she was right and nodded gratefully. But his heart continued to beat wildly.

Then the child had to pick his preschool, elementary school, elementary school cram sessions, junior high, junior high cram sessions, high school, and high school cram sessions. Then the choice to apply to colleges overseas appeared. Lao Zhang's heart once again tightened: he knew this was a good choice, but it would cost a lot more money, and it was difficult to imagine having his son thousands of miles away and not being able to protect him. Fortunately, the toddler barely glanced at the choice and waved it away.

Next he had to select his college, decide whether afterward he wanted to go to grad school, to study overseas, or to start working, choose where he wanted to work and to settle, pick a house, a car, a spouse, the engagement present, the wedding banquet, the honeymoon destination, the hospital where their child would be born, the service center that would come and help—that was as far as the choices would go, for now.

All that was left was to pick the years in which he would trade up his house, the years in which he would upgrade his car, the places he would go for vacations, the gym he would join, the retirement fund he would invest in, the frequent flier program he would sign up for. Finally, he picked a nursing home and a cemetery, and all was set.

The unselected icons hovered silently for a moment, and then gradually dimmed and went out like a sky full of stars extinguishing one after another. Flowers and confetti dropped from the ceiling, and celebratory music played. Everyone in the banquet hall cheered and clapped.

It took a while before Lao Zhang recovered, and he realized that he was soaked in sweat as though he had just emerged from a hot pool. He looked over at his wife, who was in tears. Lao Zhang waited patiently until she had calmed down a bit, and then whispered, "This is a happy occasion! Look at you . . . "

Embarrassed, his wife wiped her wet face. "Look at our son! He's so little . . . "

Lao Zhang wasn't sure he really understood her, but he felt his eyes grow hot and moist again. He shook his head. "This way is good. Good! It saves us from so much worrying."

As he spoke, he began to do the calculations in his head. The total for everything his son had chosen was going to be an astronomical sum. He and his wife would be responsible for sixty percent of it, to be paid off over thirty years. The other forty percent would be the responsibility of his son once he started working, and of course there was their son's child, and the child's child . . .

He now had a goal to strive toward for the next few decades, and a warm feeling suffused him from head to toe.

He looked back at his son. The baby remained seated in the high chair, a bowl of hot noodles symbolizing longevity in front of him. His almost translucent cheeks were flushed as he smiled like the Laughing Buddha.

New Year's Eve

Late at night, Wu was walking alone along the road. The street was empty and everything was quiet, interrupted occasionally by explosions from strings of firecrackers. The night before Chinese New Year was supposed to be spent with family, with everyone gathered around the dinner table, chatting, eating, watching the Spring Festival Gala on TV, enjoying a rare moment when the whole extended family could be together in one room.

He approached a park near home. It was even quieter here, without the daytime crowd of people practicing Tai Chi, strolling, exercising, or singing folk operas. An artificial lake lay quietly in the moonless night. Wu listened to the dull sound of gentle waves slapping against the shore and felt a chill through every pore in his skin. He turned toward a tiny pavilion next to the lake, but stopped when a dark shadow loomed before him.

"Who's there?" a shocked Wu asked.

"Who are you?"

The voice sounded familiar to Wu. Suppressing his fright, he walked closer, and realized that the other person was Lao Wang, his upstairs neighbor.

Wu let out a held breath. "You really frightened me."

"What are you doing outside at this hour?"

"I wanted to take a walk . . . to relax. What are you doing here?"

"Too many people and too much noise at home. I needed a moment of peace," Lao Wang said.

The two looked at each other, and a smile of mutual understanding appeared on their faces. Lao Wang brushed off a nearby stone bench and said, "Come, sit next to me."

Wu touched the stone, which was ice cold. "Thanks. I'd rather stand for a bit. I just ate; standing is better for digestion."

Lao Wang sighed. "New Year's . . . the older you get, the less there is to celebrate."

"Isn't that the truth. You eat, watch TV, set off some firecrackers, and then it's time to sleep. A whole year has gone by, and you've done nothing of note."

"Right," Lao Wang said. "But that's how everyone spends New Year's. I can't do anything different all by myself."

"Yeah. Everybody in the family sits down to watch the Spring Festival Gala. I'd like to do something different but I can't summon the energy. Might as well come out and walk around by myself."

"I haven't watched the Spring Festival Gala in years."

"That's pretty impressive," Wu said.

"It was easier in the past," Lao Wang said. "Singing, dancing, a few stupid skits and it's over. But now they've made it so much more difficult to avoid."

"Well, that's technological progress, right? They've developed so many new tricks."

"I don't mind if they just stick to having pop stars do their acts," Lao Wang said. "But now they insist on this 'People's Participatory Gala' business. Ridiculous."

"I can sort of see the point," said Wu. "The stars are on TV every day for the rest of the year. Might as well try something new for New Year's Eve."

"It's too much for me, all this chaos. I'd rather have a quiet, peaceful New Year's."

"But the point of New Year's is the festival mood," said Wu. "Most people like a bit of noise and atmosphere. We're not immortals in heaven, free from all earthly concerns, you know?"

"Ha! I don't think even immortals up there can tolerate this much pandemonium down here."

Both men sighed and listened to the gentle sound of the lake. After a while, Lao Wang asked, "Have you ever been picked for the Gala?"

"Of course. Twice. The first time they randomly picked my family during the live broadcast so that the whole family could appear on TV and wish everybody a happy new year. The second time was because one of my classmates had cancer. They picked him for a human-interest story, and the producer decided that it would be more tear-jerking to get the whole class and the teacher to appear with him. The Gala hosts and the audience sure cried a lot. I wasn't in too many shots, though."

"I've never been picked," said Lao Wang.

"How have you managed that?"

"I turn off the TV and go hide somewhere. The Gala has nothing to do with me."

"Why go to so much trouble? It's not a big deal to be on TV for the Gala."

"It's my nature," said Lao Wang. "I like peace and quiet. I can't stand the . . . invasiveness of it."

"Isn't that a little exaggerated?"

"Without notice, without consent, they just stick your face on TV so that everyone in the world can see you. How is that *not* invasive?"

"It's just for a few seconds. No one is going to even remember you."

"I don't like it."

"It's not as if having other people see you costs you anything."

"That's not the point. The point is *I* haven't agreed. If I agree, sure, I don't care if you follow me around with a camera twenty-four hours a day. But I don't want to be forced on there."

"I can understand your feeling," said Wu. "But it's not realistic.

Look around you! There are cameras everywhere. You can't hide for the rest of your life."

"That's why I go to places with no people."

"That's a bit extreme."

Lao Wang laughed. "I think I'm old enough to deserve not having all my choices made for me."

Wu laughed, too. "You really are a maverick."

"Hardly. This is all I can do."

White lights appeared around them, turning into a crowd of millions of faces. In the middle of the crowd was a stage, brightly lit and spectacularly decorated. Lao Wang and Wu found themselves on the stage, and loud, festive music filled their ears. A host and a hostesss approached from opposite ends of the stage.

A megawatt smile on his face, the host said, "Wonderful news, everyone! We've finally found that mythical creature: the only person in all of China who's never been on the Spring Festival Gala! Meet Mr. Wang, who lives in Longyang District."

The hostess, with an even brighter smile, added, "We have to thank this other member of the audience, Mr. Wu, who helped us locate and bring the mysterious Mr. Wang onto the stage. Mr. Wang, on this auspicious, joyous night, would you like to wish everyone a happy new year and say a few words?"

Lao Wang was stunned. It took a while for him to recover and turn to look at Wu. Wu was awkward and embarrassed, and he wanted to say something to comfort Lao Wang, but he wasn't given a chance to talk.

The host said, "Mr. Wang, this is the very first time you've been on the Gala. Can you tell us how you feel?"

Lao Wang stood up, and without saying anything, dove off the edge of the stage into the cold lake.

Wu jumped up, and his shirt was soaked with cold sweat. Blood drained from the faces of the host and the hostess. Multiple camera drones flitted through the night air, searching for Lao Wang in the lake. The millions of faces around them began to whisper and murmur, and the buzzing grew louder.

Suddenly, a ball of light appeared below the surface of the lake, and with a loud explosion, a bright, blinding light washed out everything. Wu was screaming and rolling on the ground, his clothes on fire. Finally, he managed to open his eyes and steal a peek through the cracks between his fingers: amidst the blazing white flames, a brilliant, golden pillar of light rose from the lake and disappeared among the clouds. It must have been thousands of miles long.

What the hell! thought Wu. *Is he really going back up in heaven to enjoy his peace and quiet?* Then his eyes began to burn and columns of hot smoke rose from his sockets.

The next day, the web was filled with all kinds of commentary. The explosion had destroyed all the cameras on site, and only a few fragmentary recordings of the scene could be recovered. Most of those who got to see the event live were in hospital—the explosion had damaged their hearing.

Still, everyone congratulated the Spring Festival Gala organizers for putting on the most successful program in the show's history.

Matchmaking

Xiao Li was twenty-seven. After New Year's she'd be twenty-eight. Her mother was growing worried and signed her up with a matchmaking service.

"Oh come on," said Xiao Li. "How embarrassing."

"What's embarrassing about it?" said her mother. "If I didn't use a matchmaker, where would your dad be? And where would *you* be?"

"These services are full of . . . sketchy men."

"Better than you can do on your own."

"What?" Xiao Li was incredulous. "Why?"

"They have scientific algorithms."

"Oh, you think science can guarantee good matches?"

"Stop wasting time. Are you going or not?"

And so Xiao Li put on a new dress and did her makeup, and followed her mom to a famous matchmaking service center. The manager at the service center was very enthusiastic, and asked Xiao Li to confirm her identity.

Xiao Li had no interest in being here and twisted around in her chair. "Is this going to be a lot of trouble?"

The manager smiled. "Not at all. We have the latest technology. It's super fast."

"You're asking for all my personal information. Is it safe?"

The manager continued to smile. "Please don't worry. We've been in business for years, and we've never had any problems. Not a single client has ever sued us."

Xiao Li still had more questions, but her mother had had enough. "Hurry up! Don't think you can get out of this by dragging it out."

Xiao Li put her finger on the terminal so that her prints could be scanned, and then she had a retinal scan as well so that her personal information could be downloaded to the service center's database. Next, she had to do a whole-body scan, which took three minutes.

"All set," said the manager. He reached into the terminal and pulled out a hologram that he tossed onto the floor. Xiao Li watched as a white light rose from the ground, and inside the light was a tiny figure about an inch tall, looking exactly like her and dressed in the same clothes.

The little person looked around herself and then entered a door next to her. Inside, there was a tiny table and two tiny chairs. A mini-man sat on one chair and after greeting mini-Xiao Li, the two started to talk. They spoke in a high-pitched, sped-up language and it was hard to tell what they were saying. Not even a minute later, mini-Xiao Li stood up and the two shook hands politely. Then mini-Xiao Li came out and entered the next door.

Xiao Li's mother muttered next to her. "Let's see, if it takes a minute to get to know a guy, then you can meet sixty guys in an hour. After a day, you . . . "

The still-smiling manager said, "Oh, this is only a demonstration. The real process is even faster. You don't need to wait around, of course. We'll get you the results tomorrow, guaranteed."

The manager reached out and waved his hands. The miniature men and women in the white light shrank down even further until they were tiny dots. All around them were tiny cells like a beehive, and in each cell red and green dots twitched and buzzed.

Xiao Li could no longer tell which red dot was hers, and she felt uneasy. "Is this really going to work?"

The manager assured her. "We have more than six million registered members! I'm sure you'll find your match."

"These people are . . . reliable?"

"Every member had to go through a strict screening process like the one you went through. All the information on file is one hundred percent reliable. Our dating software is the most up to date, and any match predicted by the software has always worked out in real life. If you're not satisfied, we'll refund your entire fee."

Xiao Li still hesitated, but her mother said, "Let's go. Look at you— now you're suddenly interested?"

The next afternoon, Xiao Li got a call from the manager at the matchmaking center. He explained that the software had identified 438 possible candidates: all were good looking, healthy, reliable, and shared Xiao Li's interests and values.

Xiao Li was a bit shocked. *More than four hundred?* Even if she went on a date every day, it would take more than a year to get through them all.

The manager's smile never wavered. "I suggest you try our parallel dating software and continue to get to know these men better. It takes time to know if someone will make a good spouse."

Xiao Li agreed and ten copies of mini-Xiao Li were made to go on dates with these potential matches.

Two days later, the manager called Xiao Li again. The ten mini-Xiao Lis had already gone on ten dates with each of the more than four hundred candidates, and the software had tracked and scored all the dates. The manager advised Xiao Li to aggregate the scores from the ten dates and keep only the thirty top-scorers for further consideration. Xiao Li agreed and felt more relaxed.

Three days later, the manager told Xiao Li that after further contacts and observation, seven candidates had been eliminated, five were progressing slowly in their relationships with Xiao Li, and the remaining eighteen demonstrated reciprocal satisfaction and interest. Of these eighteen, eight had already revealed their intent to marry Xiao Li, and four had shown flaws—in living habits, for instance—but were still within the acceptable range.

Xiao Li was silent. After waiting for some time, the manager gently prodded her. "It might help to ask your mother to meet them—after all, marriage is about two families coming together."

That's true. That day, Xiao Li brought her mom to the matchmaking center, and after her identity was verified, her mother was also scanned. As the dates continued, the ten mini-Xiao Lis had ten mini-moms to help as sounding boards and advisors.

Her mom's participation was very helpful, and soon only seven candidates remained. The manager said, "Miss Li, we also have software for simulating the conditions of preparing for a wedding. Why don't you try it? Many couples split up under the stress of preparing for their big day. Marriage is not something to rush into rashly."

And so the seven mini-Xiao Lis began to discuss the wedding with the seven mini-boyfriends. Relatives of all the involved couples were scanned and entered the discussion; arguments grew heated. Indeed, two of the candidates' families just couldn't come together with Xiao Li's family, and they backed out.

The manager now said, "We also have software for simulating the honeymoon. A famous writer once said the way to know if a marriage will last is to see if the couple can travel together for a whole month without hating each other."

So Xiao Li signed up for simulated honeymoons. After that, there were simulated pregnancies, simulated maternity leaves—one potential father who was only interested in holding the baby and paid no attention to Xiao Li was immediately eliminated.

Then came the simulated raising of children, simulated affairs, simulated menopause and mid-life crises, followed by simulations of various life traumas: car accidents, disability, death of a child, dying parents . . . finally the couple had to lean against each other as they entered nursing homes. Happily ever after?

Incredibly, two candidates still remained in consideration.

Xiao Li felt that after so progress, she really had to meet these two men. The manager sent her the file on the first match, and an excited Xiao Li could feel her heart beating wildly. Just as she was about to open the file, however, a warning beep sounded, and the manager's face appeared in the air.

"I'm really sorry, Miss Li. This client was also going through the simulation with another potential match, and half a minute ago, the results came out, indicating an excellent match. Given the delicacy of the situation and to avoid . . . future regrets, I suggest you not meet him just yet."

Xiao Li felt as though she had lost something. "Why didn't you tell me this earlier?"

"The whole process is automated for privacy protection. Even our staff can't monitor or intervene. But don't worry! You still have another great match."

Xiao Li admitted that advanced technology really was reliable.

She opened the file for the other match and saw his face for the first time. She felt dizzy, as though the years in their future had been compressed into this moment, concentrated, intense, overwhelming. She felt herself growing light, like a cloud about to drift into the sky.

She heard the voice of the manager. "Miss Li? Are you satisfied with our program? Would you like to arrange an in-person meeting?"

"That won't be necessary," said Xiao Li.

She showed the manager the picture. He was speechless.

"Um . . . " Xiao Li blushed. "What is your name, actually?"

"You can call me Xiao Zhao."

A month later, Xiao Li and Xiao Zhao were married.

• • •

Reunion

Yang was home from college for the Spring Festival break. Liu, a high school classmate, called to say that since it had been ten years since their graduation, he was organizing a reunion.

Yang hung up and felt nostalgic. *Has it really been ten years?*

The day was foggy and it was impossible to see anything outside the window. Yang called Liu to ask if the reunion was still on.

"Of course! The fog makes for a better atmosphere, actually."

Yang got in his car and turned on the fog navigation system. The head-up display on the windshield marked the streets and cars and pedestrians, even if he couldn't see them directly. He arrived at the gates of his old high school safely and saw that many cars were already parked along the road, some were more expensive than his, others cheaper. Yang put on the fog mask and stepped out of the car. The mask filtered the air, and the eyepiece acted as a display, allowing him to see everything hidden by the fog. He looked around and saw that the entrance to the high school was the same as he remembered: iron grille gates, a few large gilt characters in the red brick walls. The buildings and the lawn inside hadn't changed either, and as a breeze passed through, he seemed to hear the rustling of holly leaves.

Yang passed through the classroom buildings and came onto the exercise ground, where everyone used to do their morning calisthenics. A crowd was gathered there, conversing in small groups. Just about everyone in his class had arrived. Although they all wore masks, glowing faces were projected onto the masks. He examined them: most of the faces were old photographs taken during high school. Soon, a few of his best friends from that time gathered around him, and they started to talk: *Is he still in grad school? Where is he working? Has he gotten married? Has he bought a house?* The words and laughter flowed easily.

Just then, they heard a voice coming from somewhere elevated. They looked up and saw that Liu had climbed onto the rostrum. Taking a pose like their old principal, he spoke into a mike, sounding muffled: "Welcome back to our alma mater, everybody. The school is being renovated this winter, and most of the classrooms have been dismantled. That's why we have to make do with the exercise ground."

Yang was startled, and then he realized that the buildings he had passed through earlier were also nothing more than projections of old photographs. Remembering the old room where he had studied, the old cafeteria where he had eaten, and the rooftop deck where he had secretly taken naps, he wondered if any of them had survived.

Liu continued, "But this exercise ground holds a special meaning for our class. Does anyone remember why?"

The crowd was quiet. Pleased with himself, Liu lifted up something covered by a cloth. He raised his voice. "While they were renovating the exercise ground, one of the workers dug up our memory capsule. I checked: it's intact!"

He pulled off the cloth with an exaggerated motion, revealing a silver-white, square box. The crowd buzzed with excited conversation. Yang could feel his heart pounding as memories churned in his mind. At graduation, someone had suggested that each member of the class record a holographic segment, store all the recordings in a projector, and bury it under one of the trees at the edge of the exercise ground, to be replayed after ten years. This was the real reason Liu had organized the reunion.

"Do you remember how we had everyone say what they wanted to achieve in the future?" Liu asked. "Now that it's been ten years, let's take a look and see if anyone has realized their dream."

The crowd grew even more excited and started to clap.

"Since I'm holding the box, I'll start," Liu said.

He placed his hand against the box, and a small blue light came to life, like a single eye. A glowing light appeared above the box, and after a few flickers, resolved into an eighteen-year-old version of Liu.

Everyone gazed up at this youthful image of their friend and what he had chosen to remember from their high school years: there was Liu running for class president, receiving an academic and service award, representing the school on the soccer team, scoring a goal, organizing extracurricular clubs, leading his supporters in his campaign, losing the election, hearing words of encouragement from teachers and friends so that he could redouble his effort, tearfully making a speech: "Alma Mater, I'll remember you always. I will make you proud of me!"

And then, the young Liu said, "In a decade, I will have an office facing the sea!"

The light dimmed like a receding tide. The real Liu took out his phone and projected a photograph in the air: this much more mature Liu, in a suit and tie, sat behind a desk and grinned at the camera. A deep blue sea and a sky dotted with some clouds, pretty as a postcard, could be seen through the glass wall behind him.

A wave of applause. Everyone congratulated Liu on achieving his dream. Yang clapped along, but something about the scene bothered him. This didn't seem like a reunion—it was more like reality TV. But Liu had already come down from the rostrum and handed the box to someone else. Another glowing light appeared above them, and Yang couldn't help but look up with the crowd.

And so they looked at old memories: classes, tests, the flag-raising ceremony, morning exercises, being tardy, being let out of school, study hall, skipping classes, fights, smoking, breaking up . . . followed by old dreams: finding love, jobs, vacations, names, names of places, names of objects. Finally, he saw himself.

The short-cropped hair and scrawny, awkward body of his teenaged self embarrassed him, and he heard his own raspy voice: "I want to be an interesting person."

He was stunned. What had made him say such a thing back then? And how could he have no memory of saying it? But the crowd around him applauded enthusiastically and laughed, praising him for having had the audacity to say something unique.

He passed the box onto the next person, and he could feel his temples grow sweaty in the fog. He wanted this farce to be over so he could drive home, take off the mask, and take a long, hot bath.

A woman spoke next to him—he seemed to recognize the voice. He looked over. Ah, it was Ye, who had sat at the same desk with him throughout their three years in high school.

He didn't know Ye well. She was an average girl in every way: not too pretty, not too *not* pretty, not too smart, not too *not* smart. He searched through his memories and recalled that she liked to laugh, but because her teeth weren't very even, she looked a bit goofy when laughing. He recalled other bits and pieces about her: her odd gestures, her habit of doodling in their textbooks, the way she would sometimes close her eyes and press her hands against her temples and mutter. He had never asked her what she was muttering about.

He heard the eighteen-year-old Ye saying in an even, calm voice, "I don't think I have a dream. I have no idea where I'll be in ten years.

"I'm envious of each and every one of you. I'm envious that you can dream of a future. Before you had even been born, your parents had started to plan for your future. As long as you follow those plans and don't make big mistakes, you'll be fine.

"Before I was born, the doctors discovered that I had a hereditary disease. They thought I wouldn't live beyond my twentieth year. The doctors advised my mother to terminate the pregnancy. But my mother wouldn't listen to them. It became a point of friction between my parents, and eventually, they divorced.

"When I was very little, my mother told me this story. She also said, Daughter, you're going to have to rely on yourself for the rest of your life. I don't know how to help you. She also said that she would never help me make my decisions, whether it was where I wanted to play, who I wanted to be friends with, what books I wanted to buy, or what school I wanted to go to. She said that she had already made the most important decision for my life: to give birth to me. After that, whatever I decided, I didn't need her approval.

"I don't know how much longer I have. Maybe I'll die tomorrow, maybe I'll eke out a few more years. But I still haven't decided what I have to get done before I die. I'm envious of everyone who'll live longer than I because they'll have more time to think about it and more time to make it come true.

"But there are also times when I think it makes no difference whether we live longer or shorter.

"Actually, I do have dreams, many dreams. I dream of flying in a spaceship; dream of a wedding on Mars; dream of living for a long, long time so that I can see what the world will be like in a thousand, ten thousand years; dream of becoming someone great so that after I die, many people will remember my name. I also have little dreams. I dream of seeing a meteor shower; dream of having the best grade, just once, so that my mother will be happy for me; dream of a boy I like singing a song for me on my birthday; dream of catching a pickpocket trying to steal a wallet on the bus and having the courage to rush up and seize him. Sometimes, I even realize one of my dreams, but I don't know if I should be happy, don't know if I died the next day, whether I would feel that was enough, that my life was complete, perfect, and that I had no more regrets.

"I dream of seeing all of you in ten years, and hear what dreams you've realized."

She disappeared. The light dimmed bit by bit.

A moment of quiet.

Someone shouted, "But where is she?"

Yang looked down and saw that the silvery-white box was lying on the ground, surrounded by the tips of pairs of shoes. He looked around: all the faces on the masks flickered, but he couldn't tell who was who for a moment.

The crowd erupted.

"What the hell? A ghost?"

"Someone's playing a joke!"

"We went to school together for three years and I'd never heard her mention any of this. Who knows if it's true or not?"

"I've never heard of any strange disease like that."

The discussions led nowhere, and they couldn't find Ye. The reunion came to an end without a conclusion.

After dinner and some drinks, Yang drove home by himself. The fog was still heavy, and the passing, varicolored lights dissolved in the fog like pigment. He fell asleep as soon as he was in bed, but he woke up around midnight.

He was seized by a nameless terror, and he was sure that he would not see the sun rise again, that he would die during his sleep. He recalled his life, thinking about the ten years since high school that had passed far too quickly. He had once thought life rather good, like a flowery, splendid scroll, but now a rip had been torn in it, and inside was darkness, a bottomless darkness. He had fallen into a chasm from the sky, and inside the chasm was only a lightless fog. All he could see was the nothingness behind the scroll.

He curled up in the fetal position and sobbed, and he vomited his dinner onto his pillow.

The fog was gone in the morning. Yang got up and looked at the clear sky outside.

He felt refreshed, and the unpleasantness of the previous day was forgotten.

The Birthday

Grandma Zhou was almost ninety-nine, and the family planned a big celebration. But just as everything was about ready, Grandma Zhou slipped and fell in the bathroom, fracturing her foot. Although she was rushed to the hospital right away and the injury wasn't serious, it still made it hard for her to get about. She had to stay in a wheelchair all day, and she felt depressed.

The evening sky was overcast, and Grandma Zhou napped in her room by herself. Knocking noises woke her up. Raising her sleepy eyes, she saw a figure in a white dress floating in midair, indistinct, like an immortal.

"Is something happening, Young Lady?"

Young Lady wasn't a person, but the nursing home's service program. Grandma's eyesight was no longer so good, and she couldn't tell what Young Lady looked like. But she always thought she sounded like her granddaughter.

"Grandma Zhou," said Young Lady, "your family is here to celebrate your birthday!"

"What's there to celebrate? The older you grow, the more you suffer."

"Please don't say that. The young people are here because they love you. They want you to live beyond a hundred!"

Grandma Zhou was still in a bad mood, but Young Lady said, "If you keep on frowning like that, your children and grandchildren and great-grandchildren will think I haven't been taking good care of you."

Grandma Zhou thought Young Lady had taken very good care of her—in fact, she did it about as well as her real granddaughter. Her heart softened, and a smile appeared on her face.

"There we go," said a grinning Young Lady. "All right, get ready to celebrate!"

Bright lights came out of the floor and transformed the room. Grandma Zhou found herself inside a hall decorated in an antique style with red paper lanterns and red paper *Longevity* characters pasted on the walls. She was dressed in a red jacket and red pants custom made for her and sat in a carved purpleheart longevity chair, while all the guests around her also wore red. Grandma Zhou couldn't see their faces clearly, but she could hear the laughter and joyous conversations, and the noise of firecrackers going off outside was constant.

Her oldest son approached first with his family to wish her a happy birthday. There were more than a dozen people, and, after sorting themselves by generation and age, they knelt to kowtow. Grandma Zhou smiled at the children: boys, girls, some dark skinned, some fair skinned, and she had trouble saying some of their names. A few of the children were shy, and hid behind their parents to peek at her without speaking. Others were bolder, and they spoke to her in some foreign language instead of Chinese, making the adults laugh. There was also a little child curled up asleep in her mother's lap, and the mother smiled, saying, "Grandma, I'm really sorry. It's about five in the morning in our time zone."

"That's all right," said Grandma Zhou. "Children need their rest."

It took almost a quarter of an hour for the members of her oldest son's family to offer her their good wishes one by one.

Then came the family of her second son, her older daughter, her younger daughter . . . then the friends who had gone to school with her, friends from the army, the students she had taught over the years, in-laws, distant relatives . . .

Grandma Zhou had been sitting up for a long while, and her eyes were feeling tired and her throat parched. But she knew it was difficult for so many people to make time to attend her party, and so she forced herself to keep on nodding and smiling. *Advanced technology is really wonderful; it would be so much harder for them to do this in person.*

As she watched all the guests milling about the hall, she felt very moved. So many people around the globe, divided by thousands of miles, were here because of her. After all the miles she had walked and all the things she had experienced and done, she had connected all these people, many of them strangers to each other, into a web. She felt fortunate to be ninety-nine; not many people made it this far.

A figure dressed in white drifted over to her. At first she thought it was Young Lady again, but the figure knelt down and held her hand.

"Grandma, sorry I'm late. The traffic was bad."

Grandma Zhou squeezed the hands; the skin felt a bit cold, but the hands were solid. She squinted to get a closer look. It was her granddaughter who was studying overseas.

"What are you doing here?"

"To wish you a happy birthday, of course."

"You're actually here? Really here?"

"I wanted to see you."

"That's a long way to go," said Grandma Zhou.

Her granddaughter smiled. "Not that far. Not even a full day by plane."

Grandma Zhou looked her granddaughter up and down. She looked tired, but seemed to be in good spirits. Grandma Zhou smiled.

"Is it cold outside?"

"Not at all," said the granddaughter. "The moon is lovely tonight. Would you like to see it?"

"But there are still so many people here."

"Oh, that's easy to take care of," said the granddaughter.

She waved her hands, and a replica of Grandma Zhou appeared. The replica was dressed in the same red jacket and red pants, and sat in the carved purpleheart longevity chair. The guests in the hall continued to come up in waves, wishing her many years of long life and happiness.

"All right, Grandma, let's go."

The granddaughter pushed the wheelchair through the empty corridor of the nursing home until they were in the yard. There was a vigorous *shantao* tree in the middle of the yard, and to the side were a few wintersweet bushes, whose fragrance wafted on the breeze. The sky had cleared, revealing the full moon. Grandma Zhou looked at the plants in the garden and then at her granddaughter, standing tall and lovely next to her like a young poplar. *Nothing makes you realize how old you are as seeing your children's children all grown up.*

A few other residents of the nursing home were sitting under the tree, playing erhu and singing folk operas. They saw Grandma Zhou and invited her to join them.

Grandma Zhou blushed like a little girl. "I have no talent for this sort of thing at all! I've never learned to play an instrument, and I can't sing."

Lao Hu, who was playing the erhu, said, "It's just a few of us old timers trying to entertain ourselves, not the Spring Festival Gala! Lao Zhou, just perform anything you like, and we'll cheer you on. Wouldn't that be a nice way to celebrate your birthday?"

Grandma Zhou pondered this for a while, and said, "All right, I'll chant a poem for you."

Her father had taught her how to chant poems when she was little, and her father had learned from his tutor, back before the founding of the People's Republic. Back then, when children studied poetry, they didn't read it or recite it, but learned to chant along with the teacher. This was how they learned the rhythm and meter of poetry, the patterns of rhyme and tone. It was closer to singing than reading, and it sounded better.

The others quieted to listen. The moonlight was gentle like water, and everything around them seemed fresh and warm. Grandma slowed her breathing, thinking of fragments of history and tradition connected with the moon and all that is old and new around her, and began to chant:

As firecrackers send away the old year,
The spring breeze feels as warm as New Year's wine.
All houses welcome fresh sun and good cheer,
While new couplets take the place of old signs.

Originally published in Chinese in *Science Fiction World*,
June 2013.

Author's Note: While I was at my parents' home over Spring Festival break, I wanted to write some stories about ordinary lives. I don't particularly care about predicting the future, but I do think that deep changes are happening around us almost undetectably. These changes are the most real, and also the most science fictional.

The future is full of uncertainties, and it is as hard to say it will be better as it is to say it will be worse. In a few decades, I don't know if anyone will still remember how to chant ancient poems, but I do know that in every passing moment, the people in every house—men, women, old, young—are living lives as meaningful as they're ordinary.

The poem included in this story was written by the Song Dynasty poet Wang Anshi.

As an undergraduate, **Xia Jia** majored in Atmospheric Sciences at Peking University. She then entered the Film Studies Program at the Communication University of China, where she completed her Master's thesis: "A Study on Female Figures in Science Fiction Films." Recently, she obtained a Ph.D. in Comparative Literature and World Literature at Peking University, with "Chinese Science Fiction and Its Cultural Politics Since 1990⊠ as the topic of her dissertation. She now teaches at Xi'an Jiaotong University.

She has been publishing fiction since college in a variety of venues, including *Science Fiction World* and *Jiuzhou Fantasy*. Several of her stories have won the Galaxy Award, China's most prestigious science fiction award. In English translation, she has been published in *Clarkesworld* and *Upgraded*.

Falling Star

BRENDAN DuBOIS

On a late July day in Boston Falls, New Hampshire, Rick Monroe, the oldest resident of the town, sat on a park bench in the Town Common, waiting for the grocery and mail wagon to appear from Greenwich. The damn thing was supposed to arrive at two p.m., but the Congregational Church clock had just chimed three times and the road from Greenwich had remained empty. Four horses and a wagon were hitched up to a post in front of the Boston Falls General Store, some bare-chested kids were playing in the dirt road, and flies were buzzing around his face.

He stretched out his legs, saw the dirt stains at the bottom of the old overalls. Mrs. Chandler, his once-a-week house cleaner, was again doing a lousy job with the laundry, and he knew he should say something to her, but he was reluctant to do it. Having a cleaning woman was a luxury and a bad cleaning woman was better than no cleaning woman at all. Even if she was a snoop and sometimes raided his icebox and frowned whenever she reminded him of the weekly church services.

Some of the kids shouted and started running up the dirt road. He sat up, shaded his eyes with a shaking hand. There, coming down slowly, two tired horses pulling the wagon that had high wooden sides and a canvas top. He waited as the wagon pulled into the store, waited still until it was unloaded. There was really no rush, no rush at all. Let the kids have their excitement, crawling in and around the wagon. When the wagon finally pulled out, heading to the next town over, Jericho, he slowly got up, winced as his hips screamed at him. He went across the cool grass and then the dirt road, and up to the wooden porch. The children moved away from him, except for young Tom Cooper, who stood there, eyes wide open. Glen Roundell, the owner of the General Store and one of the town's three selectmen, came up to him with a paper sack and a small packet of envelopes, tied together with a piece of twine.

"Here you go, Mister Monroe," he said, his voice formal, wearing a starched white shirt, black tie and white store apron that reached the floor. "Best we can do this week. No beef, but there is some bacon there. Should keep if you get home quick enough."

"Thanks, Glen," he said. "On account, all right?"

Glen nodded. "That's fine."

He turned to step off the porch, when a man stepped out of the shadows. Henry Cooper, Tom's father, wearing a checked flannel shirt and blue jeans, his thick black beard down to mid-chest. "Would you care for a ride back to your place, Mister Monroe?"

He shifted the bag in his hands, smiled. "Why, that would be grand." And he was glad that Henry had not come into town with his wife, Marcia, for even though she was quite active in the church, she had some very un-Christian thoughts towards her neighbors, especially an old man like Rick Monroe, who kept to himself and wasn't a churchgoer.

Rick followed Henry and his boy outside, and he clambered up on the rear, against a couple of wooden boxes and a barrel. Henry said, "You can sit up front, if you'd like," and Rick said, "No, that's your boy's place. He can stay up there with you."

Henry unhitched his two-horse team, and in a few minutes, they were heading out on the Town Road, also known as New Hampshire Route 12. The rear of the wagon jostled and was bumpy, but he was glad he didn't have to walk it. It sometimes took him nearly an hour to walk from home to the center of town, and he remembered again—like he had done so many times—how once in his life it only took him ninety minutes to travel thousands of miles.

He looked again at the town common, at the stone monuments clustered there, commemorating the war dead from Boston Falls, those who had fallen in the Civil War, Spanish-American War, World Wars I and II, Korea, Vietnam, and even the first and second Gulf Wars. Then, the town common was out of view, as the horse and wagon made its way out of a small New Hampshire village, hanging on in the sixth decade of the twenty-first century.

When the wagon reached his home, Henry and his boy came down to help him, and Henry said, "Can I bring some water out for the horses? It's a dreadfully hot day," and Rick said, "Of course, go right ahead." Henry nodded and said, "Tom, you help Mister Monroe in with his groceries. You do that."

"Yes, sir," the boy said, taking the bag from his hands, and he was embarrassed at how he enjoyed being helped. The inside of the house was cool—but not cool enough, came a younger voice from inside, a voice that said, remember when you could set a switch and have it cold enough to freeze your toes?—and he walked into the dark kitchen, past the coal-burning stove. From the grocery sack he took out a few canned goods—their labels in black and white, glued sloppily on—and the wax paper with the bacon inside. He went to the icebox, popped it open quickly and shut it. Tom was there, looking on, gazing around the room, and he knew what the boy was looking at: the framed photos of the time when Rick was younger and stronger, just like the whole damn country.

"Tom?"

"Yessir?"

"Care for a treat?"

Tom scratched at his dirty face with an equally dirty hand. "Momma said I shouldn't take anything from strangers. Not ever."

Rick said, "Well, boy, how can you say I'm a stranger? I live right down the road from you, don't I?"

"Unh-hunh."

"Then we're not strangers. You sit right there and don't move."

Tom clambered up on a wooden kitchen chair and Rick went over to the counter, opened up the silverware drawer, took out a spoon. Back to the icebox he went, this time opening up the freezer compartment, and he quickly pulled out a small white coffee cup with a broken handle. He placed the cold coffee cup down on the kitchen table and gave the boy the spoon.

"Here, dig in," he said.

Tom looked curious but took the spoon and scraped against the ice-like confection in the bottom of the cup. He took a taste and his face lit up, like a lightbulb behind a dirty piece of parchment. The next time the spoon came up it was nearly full, and Tom quickly ate everything in the cup, and then licked the spoon and tried to lick the inside of the cup.

"My, that was good!" he said. "What was it, Mister Monroe?"

"Just some lemonade and sugar, frozen up. Not bad, hunh?"

"It was great! Um, do you have any more? Sir?"

Rick laughed, thinking of how he had made it this morning, for a dessert after dinner. Not for a boy not even ten, but so what? "No, 'fraid not. But come back tomorrow. I might have some then, if I can think about it."

At the kitchen sink he poured water into the cup, and the voice returned. Why not, it said. Tell the boy what he's missing. Tell him how it was like, back when a kid his age would laugh rather than eat frozen, sugary lemonade. That with the change in his pocket, he could walk outside and meet up with an ice cream cart that sold luxuries unknown today in the finest restaurants. Tell him that, why don't you?

He coughed and turned, saw Tom was looking up again at the photos. "Mister Monroe . . . "

"Yes?"

"Mister Monroe, did you really go to the stars? Did you?"

Rick smiled, glad to see the curiosity in the boy's face, and not fear. "Well, I guess I got as close as anyone could, back then. You see—"

The boy's father yelled from outside. "Tom! Time to go! Come on out!"

Rick said, "Guess you have to listen to your dad, son. Tell you what, next time you come back, I'll tell you everything you want to know. Deal?"

The boy nodded and ran out of the kitchen. His hips were still aching and he thought about lying down, before going through the mail, but he made his way outside, where Tom was up on the wagon. Henry came up and offered his hand, and Rick shook it, glad that Henry wasn't one to try the strength test with someone as old as he. Henry said, "Have a word with you, Mister Monroe?"

"Sure," he said. "But only if you call me Rick."

From behind the thick beard, he thought he could detect a smile. "All right . . . Rick."

They both sat down on old wicker rocking chairs and Henry said, "I'll get right to it, Rick."

"Okay."

"There's a town meeting tonight. I think you should go."

"Why?"

"Because . . . well, there's some stirrings. That's all. About a special committee being set up. A morals committee, to ensure that only the right people live here in Boston Falls."

"And who decides who are the right people?" he asked, finding it hard to believe this conversation was actually taking place.

Henry seemed embarrassed. "The committee and the selectmen, I guess . . . you see, there's word down south, about some of the towns there, they still got trouble with refugees and transients rolling in from Connecticut and New York. Some of those towns, the natives, they're being overwhelmed, outvoted, and they're not the same anymore. And since you, um—"

"I was born here, Henry. You know that. Just because I lived someplace else for a long time, that's held against me?"

"Well, I'm just sayin' it's not going to help . . . with what you did back then, and the fact you don't go to church, and other things, well . . . it might be worthwhile if you go there. That's all. To defend yourself."

Even with the hot weather, Rick was feeling a cold touch upon his hands. Now we're really taking a step back, he thought. Like the Nuremberg laws, in Nazi Germany. Ensuring that only the ethnically and racially pure get to vote, to shop, to live . . .

"And if this committee decides you don't belong? What then? Arrested? Exiled? Burnt at the stake?"

Now his neighbor looked embarrassed as he stepped up from the wicker chair. "You should just be there, Mister uh, I mean, Rick. It's at eight o'clock. At the town hall."

"That's a long walk in, when it's getting dark. Any chance I could get a ride?"

Even with his neighbor's back turned to him, Rick could sense the humiliation. "Well, I, well, I don't think so, Rick. I'm sorry. You see, I think Marcia wants to visit her sister after the meeting, and I don't know what time we might get back, and, well, I'm sorry."

Henry climbed up into the wagon, retrieved the reins from his son, and Rick called out. "Henry?"

"Yes?"

"Any chance your wife is on this committee?"

The expression on his neighbor's face was all he needed to know, as the wagon turned around on his brown lawn and headed back up to the road.

Back inside, he grabbed his mail and went upstairs, to the spare bedroom that he had converted into an office, during the first year he had made it back to Boston Falls. He went to unlock the door and found that it was already open. Damn his memory, which he knew was starting to show its age, just like his hips. He was certain he had locked it the last time. He sat down at the desk and untied the twine, knowing he would save it. What was that old Yankee saying? Use it up, wear it out, or do without? Heavy thrift, one of the many lessons being re-learned these years.

One envelope he set aside to bring into Glen Roundell, the General Store owner. It was his Social Security check, only three months late, and Glen—who was also the town's banker—would take it and apply it against Rick's account. Not much being made for sale nowadays, whatever tiny amount his Social Security check was this month was usually enough to keep his account in good shape.

There was an advertising flyer for the Grafton County Fair, set to start next week. Another flyer announcing a week-long camp revival at the old Boy Scout camp on Conway Lake, during the same time. Competition, no doubt. And a thin envelope, postmarked Houston, Texas, which he was happy to see. It had only taken a month for the envelope to get here, which he thought was a good sign. Maybe some things were improving in the country.

Maybe.

He slit open the envelope with an old knife, saw the familiar handwriting inside.

Dear Rick,

Hope this sees you doing well in the wilds of New Hampshire.

Down here what passes for recovery continues. Last month, two whole city blocks had their power restored. It only comes on for a couple of hours a day, and no a/c is allowed, but it's still progress, eh?

Enclosed are the latest elements for Our Boy. I'm sorry to say the orbit degradation is continuing. Latest guess is that Our Boy may be good for another five years, maybe six.

Considering what was spent in blood and treasure to put him up there, it breaks my heart.

If you get bored and lonely up there, do consider coming down here. I understand that with Amtrak coming back, it should only take four weeks to get here. The heat is awful but at least, you'll be in good company with those of us who still remember.

Your pal,
Brian

With the handwritten sheet was another sheet of paper, with a listing of dates and times, and he shook his head in dismay. Most of the sightings were for early mornings, and he hated getting up in the morning. But tonight—how fortunate!—there was going to be a sighting at just after eight o'clock.

Eight o'clock. Why did that sound familiar?

Now he remembered. The town meeting tonight, where supposedly his fate and those of any other possible sinners was to be decided. He carefully folded up the letter, put it back in the envelope. He decided one more viewing was more important, more important than whatever chatter session was going to happen later. And besides, knowing what he did about the town and its politics, the decision had already been made.

He looked around his small office, with the handmade bookshelves and books, and more framed photos on the cracked plaster wall. One of the photos was of he and his friend, Brian Poole, wearing blue zippered jumpsuits, standing in front of something large and complex, built ages ago in the swamps of Florida.

"Thanks, guy," he murmured, and he got up and went downstairs, to think of what might be for dinner.

Later that night he was in the big backyard, a pasture that he let his other neighbor, George Thompson, mow for hay a couple of times each summer, for which George gave him some venison and smoked ham over the long winters in exchange. He brought along a folding lawn chair, its bright plastic cracked and faded away, and he sat there, stretching out his legs. It was a quiet night, like every night since he had come here, years ago. He smiled in the darkness. What strange twists of fate and fortune had brought him back here, to his old family farm. He had grown up here, until his dad had moved the family south, to a suburb of Boston, and from there, high school and Air Force ROTC, and then many, many years traveling, thousands upon thousands of miles, hardly ever thinking about the old family farm, now owned by a second or third family. And he would have never come back here, until the troubles started, when—

A noise made him turn his head. Something crackling out there, in the underbrush.

"Who's out there?" he called out, wondering if some of the more hot-blooded young'uns in town had decided not to wait until the meeting was over. "Come out and show yourself."

A shape came out from the woodline, ambled over, small and then there was a young boy's voice, "Mister Monroe, it's me, Tom Cooper."

"Tom? Oh, yes, Tom. Come on over here."

The young boy came up, sniffling some, and Rick said, "Tom, you gave me a bit of a surprise. What can I do for you?"

Tom stood next to him, and said slowly, "I was just wondering . . . well, that cold stuff you gave me earlier, that tasted really good. I didn't know if you had any more left . . . "

He laughed. "Sorry, guy. Maybe tomorrow. How come you're not with your mom and dad at the meeting?"

Tom said, "My sister Ruth is suppose to be watching us, but I snuck out of my room and came here. I was bored."

"Well, boredom can be good, if it means something will happen. Tell you what, Tom, wait a couple of minutes, I'll show you something special."

"What's that?"

"You just wait and I'll show you."

Rick folded his hands together in his lap, looked over at the southeast. Years and years ago, that part of the night sky would be a light yellow glow, the lights from the cities in that part of the state. Now, like every other part of the night sky, there was just blackness and the stars, the night sky now back where it had once been, almost two centuries ago.

There. Right there. A dot of light, moving up and away from the horizon.

"Take a look, Tom. See that moving light?"

"Unh-hunh."

"Good. Just keep your eye on it. Look at it go."

The solid point of light rose up higher and seemed brighter, and he found his hands were tingling and his chest was getting tighter. Oh God, how beautiful, how beautiful it had been up there, looking down on the great globe, watching the world unfold beneath you, slow and majestic and lovely, knowing that as expensive and ill-designed and over-budget and late in being built, it was there, the first permanent outpost for humanity, the first step in reaching out to the planets and stars that were humanity's destiny . . .

The crickets seemed louder. An owl out in the woods hoo-hoo'ed, and beside him, Tom said, "What is it, Mister Monroe?"

The light seemed to fade some, and then it disappeared behind some tall pines, and Rick found that his eyes had gotten moist. He wiped at them and said, "What do you think it was?"

"I dunno. I sometimes see lights move at night, and momma tells me that it's the Devil's work, and I shouldn't look at 'em. Is that true?"

He rubbed at his chin, thought for a moment about just letting the boy be, let him grow up with his illusions and whatever misbegotten faith his mother had put in his head, let him think about farming and hunting and fishing, to concentrate on what was real, what was necessary, which was getting enough food to eat and a warm place and—

No! the voice inside him shouted. No, that's not fair, to condemn this boy and the others to a life of peasantry, just because of some wrong things that had been done, years before the child was even born. He shook his head and said, "Well, I can see why some people would think it's the Devil's work, but the truth is, Tom, that was a building up there. A building made by men and women and put up in the sky, more than a hundred miles up."

Tom sounded skeptical. "Then how come it doesn't fall down?"

Great, the voice said. Shall we give him a lecture about Newton? What do you suggest?

He thought for a moment and said, "It's complex, and I don't want to bore you, Tom. But trust me, it's up there. In fact, it's still up there and will be for a while. Even though nobody's living in it right now."

Tom looked up and said, "Where is it now?"

"Oh, I imagine it's over Canada by now. You see, it goes around the whole globe in what's called an orbit. Only takes about ninety minutes or so."

Tom seemed to think about that and said shyly, "My dad. He once said you were something. A spaceman. That you went to the stars. Is that true?"

"True enough. We never made it to the stars, though we sure thought about it a lot."

"He said you flew up in the air. Like a bird. And the places you went, high enough, you had to carry your own air with you. Is that true, too?"

"Yes, it is."

"Jeez. You know, my momma, well . . . "

"Your momma, she doesn't quite like me, does she?"

"Unh-hunh. She says you're not good. You're unholy. And some other stuff."

Rick thought about telling the boy the truth about his mother, decided it could wait until the child got older. God willing, the boy would learn soon enough about his mother. Aloud Rick said, "I'm going back to my house. Would you like to get something?"

"Another cold treat?" came the hopeful voice.

"No, not tonight. Maybe tomorrow. Tonight, well, tonight I want to give you something that'll last longer than any treat."

A few minutes later they were up in his office, Tom talking all the while about the fishing he had done so far this summer, the sleep-outs in the back pasture, and about his cousin Lloyd, who lived in the next town over, Hancock, and who died of something called polio. Rick shivered at the matter of fact way Tom had mentioned his cousin's death. A generation ago, a death like that would have never happened. Hell, a generation ago, if somebody of Tom's age had died, the poor kid would have been shoved into counseling sessions and group therapies, trying to get closure about the damn thing. And now? Just part of growing up.

In his office Tom ooh'ed and aaah'ed over the photos on his wall, and Rick explained the best he could of what they were about. "Well, that's the dot of light we just saw. It's actually called a space station. Over there, that's what you used to fly up to the space station. It's called a space shuttle. Or a rocket, if you prefer. This . . . this is a picture of me, up in the space station."

"Really?" Tom asked. "You were really there?"

He found he had to sit down, so he did, his damn hips aching something fierce. "Yes, I was really up there. One of the last people up there, to tell you the truth, Tom. Just before, well . . . just before everything changed."

Tom stood before a beautiful photo of a full moon, the craters and mountains and flat seas looking as sharp as if they were made yesterday. He said, "Momma said that it was God who punished the world back then, because men were evil, because they ignored God. Is that true, Mister Monroe? What really happened back then?"

His fists suddenly clenched, as if powered by memory. Where to begin, young man, he thought. Where to begin. Let's talk about a time when computers were in everything, from your car to your toaster to your department store cash register. Everything linked up and interconnected. And when the systems are getting more and more complex, the childish ones, the vandals, the destructive hackers, they have to prove that they have the knowledge and skills and wherewithal to take down a system. Oh, the defenses grew stronger and stronger, as did the viruses, and the evil ones redoubled their efforts, like the true Vandals coming into Rome, burning and destroying something that somebody else created. The defenses grew more in-depth, the attacks more determined, until one bright soul—if such a creature could be determined to have a soul—came up with ultimate computer virus. No, not one that wormed its way into software through backdoors or anything fancy like that. Nossir. This virus was one that attacked the hardware, the platforms, that spread—God knows how—theories ranged from human touch to actual impulses over fiber optics—and destroyed the chips. That's all. Just ate the chips and left burnt-out crumbs behind, so that in days, almost every thing in the world that used a computer was silent, dark and dead.

Oh, he was a smart one—for the worst of the hackers were always male—whoever he was, and Rick often wished that the designer of the ultimate virus (called the Final Virus, for a very good reason) had been on an aircraft or an operating room table when it had struck. For when the computers sputtered out and died, the chaos that was unleashed upon the world . . . Cars, buses, trains, trucks. Dead, not moving. Hundreds of thousands of people, stranded far from home. Aircraft falling out of the skies. Ships at sea, slowly drifting, unable to maneuver. Stock markets, banks, corporations, everything and any thing that stored the wealth of a nation in electronic impulses, silent. All the interconnections that fed and clothed and fueled and protected and sheltered most of the world's billions had snapped apart, like brittle rubber bands. Within days the cities had become uninhabitable, as millions streamed into the countryside. Governments wavered and collapsed. Communications were sparse, for networks and radio stations and the cable stations were off the air as well. Rumors and fear spread like a plague itself, and the Four Horsemen of the Apocalypse—called out from retirement at last—swept through almost the entire world.

There were a few places that remained untouched: Antarctica and a few remote islands. But for the rest of the world . . . sometimes the only light on the nightside of the planet were the funeral pyres, where the bodies were being burnt.

He grew nauseous, remembering what had happened to him and how it took him months to walk back here, to his childhood home, and he repressed the memory of eating something a farmer had offered him—it hadn't exactly looked like dog, but God, he had been so hungry—and he looked over to young Tom. How could he even begin to tell such a story to such an innocent lad?

He wouldn't. He composed himself and said, "No, God didn't punish us back then. We did. It was a wonderful world, Tom, a wonderful place. It wasn't perfect and many people did ignore God, did ignore many good things . . . but we did things. We fed people and cured them and some of us, well, some of us planned to go to the stars."

He went up to the wall, took down the picture of the International Space Station, the Big Boy himself, and pointed it out to Tom. "Men and women built that on the ground, Tom, and brought it up into space. They did it for good, to learn things, to start a way for us to go back to the moon and to Mars. To explore. There was no evil there. None."

Tom looked at the picture and said, "And that's the dot of light we saw? Far up in the sky?"

"Yes."

"And what's going to happen to it?"

He looked at the framed photo, noticed his hands shaking some. He put the photo back up on the wall. "One of these days, it's going to get lower and lower. It just happens. Things up in orbit can't stay up there forever. Unless somebody can go up there and do something . . . it'll come crashing down."

He sat down in the chair, winced again at the shooting pains in his hips. There was a time when he could have had new hips, new knees, or—if need be—new kidneys, but it was going to take a long time for those days to ever come back. From his infrequent letters from Brian, he knew that work was still continuing in some isolated and protected labs, to find an answer to the Final Virus. But with people starving and cities still unlit, most of the whole damn country had fallen back to the late 1800s, when power was provided by muscles, horses, or steam. Computers would just have to wait.

Tom said, "I hope it doesn't happen, Mister Monroe. It sounds really cool."

Rick said, "Well, maybe when you grow up, if you're really smart, you can go up there and fix it. And think about me when you're doing it. Does that sound like fun?"

The boy nodded and Rick remembered why he had brought the poor kid up here. He got out of his chair, went over to his bookshelf, started moving around the thick volumes and such, until he found a slim book, a book he had bought once for a future child, for one day he had promised Kathy Meserve that once he left the astronaut corps, he would marry her . . . . Poor Kathy, in London on a business trip, whom he had never seen or heard from, ever again, after the Final Virus had broken out.

He came over to Tom and gave him the book. It was old but the cover was still bright, and it said, MY FIRST BOOK ON SPACE TRAVEL. Rick said, "You can read, can't you?"

"Unh-hunh, I sure can."

"Okay." He rubbed at the boy's head, not wanting to think of Kathy Meserve or the children he never had. "You take this home and read it. You can learn a lot about the stars and planets and what it was like, to explore space and build the first space station. Maybe you can get back up there, Tom." Or your children's children, he thought, but why bring that depressing thought up. "Maybe you can be what I was, a long time ago."

Tom's voice was solemn. "A star man?"

Rick shook his head. "No, nothing fancy like that. An astronaut. That's all. Look, it's getting late. Why don't you head home."

And the young boy ran from his office, holding the old book in his hands, as if scared Rick was going to change his mind and take it away from him.

● ● ●

It was the sound of the horses that woke him, neighing and moving about in his yard, early in the morning. He got out of bed, cursed his stiff joints, and slowly got dressed. At the foot of the bed was a knapsack, for he knew a suitcase would not work. He picked up the knapsack—which he had put together last night—and walked downstairs, walked slowly, as he noticed the woodwork and craftsmanship that a long forgotten great-great-great grandfather had put into building this house, which he was now leaving.

He went out on the front porch, shaded his eyes from the hot morning sun. There were six or seven horses in his front yard, three horse-drawn wagons, and a knot of people in front. Some children were clustered out under the maple tree by the road, their parents no doubt telling them to stay away. He recognized all of the faces in the crowd, but was pleased to see that Glen Roundell, the store owner and one of the three selectmen, was not there, as well as Henry Cooper, but Henry's wife Marcia was there, thin-lipped and perpetually angry, and she strode forward, holding something at her side. She wore a long cotton skirt and long-sleeve shirt—and that insistent voice inside his head wondered why again, with technology having tumbled two hundred years, why did fashion have to follow suit?—and she announced loudly, "Rick Monroe, you know why we're here, don't you."

"Mrs. Cooper, I'm sure I have some idea, but why don't you inform me, in case I'm mistaken. I know that of your many fine attributes, correcting the mistakes of others is your finest."

She looked around the crowd, as if seeking their support, and she pressed on, even though there was a smile or two at his comment. "At a special town meeting last night, it was decided by a majority of the town to suspend your residency here, in Boston Falls, due to your past crimes and present immorality."

"Crimes?" In the crowd he noticed a man in a faded and patched uniform, and he said, "Chief Godin. You know me. What crimes have I committed?"

Chief Sam Godin looked embarrassed. A kid of about twenty-two or thereabouts, he was the Chief because he had strong hands and was a good shot. The uniform shirt he wore was twice as old as he was, but he wore it proudly, since it represented his office.

Today, though, he looked like he would rather be wearing anything else. He seemed to blush and said, "Gee, Mister Monroe . . . no crimes here, since you've moved back. But there's been talk of what you did, back then, before . . . before the change. You were a scientist or something. Worked with computers. Maybe had something to do with the change, that's the kind of crimes that we were thinking about."

Rick sighed. "Very good. That's the crime I've been accused of, of being educated. That I can accept. But immoral? Where's your proof?"

"Right here," Marcia Cooper said triumphantly. "See? This old magazine, with depraved photos and lustful women . . . kept in your house, to show any youngster that came by. Do you deny having this in your possession?"

And despite it all, he felt like laughing, for Mrs. Cooper was holding up—and holding up tight so nothing inside would be shown, of course—an ancient copy of *Playboy* magazine. The damn thing had been in his office, and sometimes he would just glance though the slick pages and sigh at a world—and a type of woman—long gone. Then something came to him and he saw another woman in the crowd, arms folded tight, staring in distaste towards him. It all clicked.

"No, I don't deny it," Rick said, "and I also don't deny that Mrs. Chandler, for once in her life, did a good job cleaning my house. Find anything else in there, Mrs. Chandler, you'd like to pass on to your neighboors?"

She just glared, said nothing. He looked up at the sun. It was going to be another hot day.

The Chief stepped forward and said, "We don't want any trouble, Mister Monroe. But it's now the law. You have to leave."

He picked up his knapsack, shrugged his arms through the frayed straps, almost gasped at the heavy weight back there. "I know."

The Chief said, "If you want, I can get you a ride to one of the next towns over, save you—"

"No," he said, not surprised at how harsh he responded. "No, I'm not taking any of your damn charity. By God years ago I walked into this town alone, and I'll walk out of this town alone as well."

Which is what he started to do, coming down the creaky steps, across the unwatered lawn. The crowd in front of him slowly gave way, like they were afraid he was infected or some damn thing. He looked at their dirty faces, the ignorant looks, the harsh stares, and he couldn't help himself. He stopped and said, "You know, I pity you. If it hadn't been for some unknown clown, years ago, you wouldn't be here. You'd be on a powerboat in a lake. You'd be in an air-conditioned mall, shopping. You'd be talking to each other over frozen drinks on where to fly to vacation this winter. That's what you'd be doing."

Marcia Cooper said, "It was God's will. That's all."

Rick shook his head. "No, it was some idiot's will, and because of that, you've grown up to be peasants. God save you and your children."

They stayed silent but he noticed that some of the younger men were looking fidgety, and were sparing glances to the Chief, like they were wondering if the Chief would intervene if they decided to stone him or some damn thing. Time to get going, and he tried not to think of the long miles that were waiting for him. Just one step after another, that's all. Maybe, if his knees and hips held together, he could get to the train station in Concord. Maybe. Take Brian up on his offer. He made it out to the dirt road, decided to head left, up to Greenwich, for he didn't want to walk through town. Why tempt fate?

He turned and looked one last time at his house, and then looked over to the old maple tree, where some of the children, bored by what had been going on, were now scurrying around the tree trunk.

But not all of the children.

One of them was by himself, at the road's edge. He looked nervous, and he raised his shirt, and even at this distance, he could make out young Tom Cooper, standing there, his gift of a book hidden away in the waistband of his jeans. Tom lowered his shirt and then waved, and Rick, surprised, smiled and waved back.

And then he turned his back on his home and his town, and started walking away.

First published in *Space Stations,* edited by Martin Greenberg and John Helfers, 2010.

ABOUT THE AUTHOR

Brendan DuBois has twice received the Shamus Award from the Private Eye Writers of America, been nominated three times for the Edgar Allan Poe Award given by the Mystery Writers of America, and has had stories reprinted in *The Best American Mystery Stories of the Century* and *The Best American Noir of the Century.* Hes the author of sixteen novels and over one hundred and thirty short stories. His science fiction novels include *Resurrection Day* and *Six Days.* His most recent novel is *Deadly Cove,* part of the "Lewis Cole" mystery series, which also includes *Dead Sand, Black Tide, Shattered Shell, Killer Waves,* and *Buried Dreams.* He is also a "Jeopardy!" gameshow champion. He lives in Exeter, NH with his family.

Her Furry Face
LEIGH KENNEDY

Douglas was embarrassed when he saw Annie and Vernon mating.

He'd seen hours of sex between orangutans, but this time was different. He'd never seen *Annie* doing it. He stood in the shade of the pecan tree for a moment, iced tea glasses sweating in his hand, shocked, then he backed around the comer of the brick building. He was confused. The cicadas seemed louder than usual, the sun hotter, and the squeals of pleasure from the apes strange.

He walked back to the front porch and sat down. His mind still saw the two giant mounds of red-orange fur moving together like one being.

When the two orangs came back around, Douglas thought he saw smugness in Vernon's face. Why not, he thought? I guess I would be smug, too.

Annie flopped down on the grassy front yard and crossed one leg over the other, her abdomen bulging high; she gazed upward into the heavy white sky.

Vernon bounded toward Douglas. He was young and red-chocolate-colored. His face was still slim, without the older orangutan jowls yet.

"Be polite," Douglas warned him.

"Drink tea, please?" Vernon signed rapidly, the fringe on his elbows waving. "Dry as bone."

Douglas handed Vernon one of the glasses of tea, though he'd brought it out for Annie. The handsome nine-year-old downed it in a gulp. "Thank you," he signed. He touched the edge of the porch and withdrew his long fingers. "Could fry egg," he signed, and instead of sitting, swung out hand-over-hand on the ropes between the roof of the schoolhouse and the trees. It was a sparse and dry substitute for the orang's native rain forest.

He's too young and crude for Annie, Douglas thought.

"Annie," Douglas called. "Your tea."

Annie rolled onto one side and lay propped on an elbow, staring at him. She was lovely. Fifteen-years-old, her fur was glossy and coppery, her small yellow eyes in the fleshy face expressive and intelligent. She started to rise up toward him, but turned toward the road.

The mail jeep was coming down the highway.

In a blurred movement, she set off at a four-point gallop down the half-mile drive toward the mailbox. Vernon swung down from his tree and followed, giving a small groan.

Reluctant to go out in the sun, Douglas put down the tea anyway and followed the apes along the drive. By the time he got near them, Annie was sitting with mail sorted between her toes, holding an opened letter in her hands. She looked up with an expression on her face that he'd never seen—it could have been fear, but it wasn't.

She handed the letter to Vernon, who pestered her for it. "Douglas," she signed, "they want to buy my story."

Therese lay in the bathwater, her knees sticking up high, her hair floating beside her face. Douglas sat on the edge of the tub; as he talked to her he was conscious that he spoke a double language—the one with his lips and the other with his hands.

"As soon as I called Ms. Young, the magazine editor, and told her who Annie was, she got really excited. She asked me why we hadn't sent a letter explaining it with the story, so I told her that Annie didn't want anyone to know first."

"Did Annie decide that?" Therese sounded skeptical, as she always seemed to when Douglas talked about Annie.

"We talked about it and she wanted it that way." Douglas felt the resistance from Therese. Why she never understood, he didn't know, unless she did it to provoke him. She acted as though she thought an ape was still just an ape, no matter what he or she could do. "Anyway," he said, "she talked about doing a whole publicity thing to the hilt—talk shows, autograph parties. You know. But Dr. Morris thinks it would be better to keep things quiet."

"Why?" Therese sat up; her legs went underwater and she soaped her arms.

"Because she'd be too nervous. Annie, I mean. It might disrupt her education to become a celebrity. Too bad. Even Dr. Morris knows that it would be great for fundraising. But I guess we'll let the press in some."

Therese began to shampoo her hair. "I brought home that essay that Sandy wrote yesterday. The one I told you about. Now if she were an orangutan instead of just a deaf kid, she could probably get it published in *Fortune*." Therese smiled.

Douglas stood. He didn't like the way Therese headed for the old argument—no matter what one of Therese's deaf students did, if Annie could do it one one-hundredth as well, it was more spectacular. Douglas knew it was true, but why Therese was so bitter about it, he didn't understand.

"That's great," he said, trying to sound enthusiastic.

"Will you wash my back?" she asked.

He crouched and absent-mindedly washed her. "I'll never forget Annie's face when she read that letter."

"Thank you," Therese said. She rinsed. "Do you have any plans for this evening?"

"I've got work to do," he said, leaving the bathroom. "Would you like me to work in the bedroom so you can watch television?"

After a long pause, she said "No, I'll read."

He hesitated in the doorway. "Why don't you go to sleep early? You look tired."

She shrugged. "Maybe I am."

In the playroom at the school, Douglas watched Annie closely. It was still morning, though late. In the recliner across the room from him, she seemed a little sleepy. Staring out the window, blinking, she marked her place in Pinkwater's *Fat Men From Space* with a long brown finger.

He had been thinking about Therese, who'd been silent and morose that morning. Annie was never morose, though often quiet. He wondered if Annie was quiet today because she sensed that Douglas was not happy. When he'd come to work, she'd given him an extra hug.

He wondered if Annie could have a crush on him, like many schoolgirls have on their teachers. Remembering her mating with Vernon days before, he idly wandered into a fantasy of touching those petals of her genitals and gently, gently moving inside her.

The physical reaction to his fantasy embarrassed him. *God, what am I thinking?* He shook himself out of the reverie, averting his gaze for a few moments, until he'd gotten control of himself again.

"Douglas," Annie signed. She walked erect, towering, to him and sat down on the floor at his feet. Her flesh folded into her lap like dough.

"What?" he asked, wondering suddenly if orangutans were telepathic.

"Why you say my story children's?"

He looked blankly at her.

"Why not send *Harper's*?" she asked, having to spell out the name of the magazine.

He repressed a laugh, knowing it would upset her. "It's . . . it's the kind of story children would like."

"Why?"

He sighed. "The level of writing is . . . *young*. Like you, sweetie." He stroked her head, looking into the small, intense eyes. "You'll get more sophisticated as you grow."

"I smart as you," she signed. "You understand me always because I talk smart. You not always talk smart."

Douglas was dumbfounded by her logic.

She tilted her head and waited. When Douglas shrugged, she seemed to assume victory and returned to her recliner.

Dr. Morris came in. "Here we go," she said, handing him the paper and leaving again.

Douglas skimmed the page until he came to an article about the "ape author." He scanned it. It contained one of her flashpoints; this and the fact that she was irritable from being in estrus made him consider hiding it. But that wouldn't be right.

"Annie," he said softly.

She looked up.

"There's an article about you."

"Me read," she signed, putting her book on the floor. She came and crawled up on the sofa next to him. He watched her eyes as they jerked across every word. He grew edgy. She read on.

Suddenly she took off as if from a diving board. He ran after her as she bolted out the door. The stuffed dog which had always been a favorite toy was being shredded in those powerful hands even before he knew she had it. Annie screamed as she pulled the toy apart, running into the yard.

Terrified by her own aggression, she ran up the tree with stuffing falling like snow behind her.

Douglas watched as the shade filled with foam rubber and fake fur. The tree branches trembled. After a long while, she stopped pummeling the tree and sat quietly.

She spoke to herself with her long ape hand. "Not animal," she said, "not animal."

Douglas suddenly realized that Therese was afraid of the apes.

She watched warily as the four of them strolled along the edge of the school acreage. Douglas knew that Therese didn't appreciate the grace of Annie's muscular gait as he did; the sign language that passed between them was as similar to the Ameslan that Therese used for her deaf children as British to Jamaican. Therese couldn't appreciate Annie in creative conversation.

It wasn't good to be afraid of the apes, no matter how educated they were.

He had invited her out, hoping it would please her to be included in his world here. She had only visited briefly twice before.

Vernon lagged behind them, snapping pictures now and then with his expensive but hardy camera modified for his hands. Vernon took several pictures of Annie and one of Douglas, but only when Therese had separated from him to peer in between the rushes at the edge of the creek.

"Annie," Douglas called, pointing ahead. "A cardinal. The red bird."

Annie lumbered forward. She glanced back to see where Douglas pointed, then stood still, squatting. Douglas walked beside her and they watched the bird.

It flew.

"Gone," Annie signed.

"Wasn't it pretty, though?" Douglas asked.

They ambled on. Annie stopped often to investigate shiny bits of trash or large bugs. They rarely came this far from the school. Vernon whizzed past them, a dark auburn streak of youthful energy.

Remembering Therese, Douglas turned. She sat on a stump far behind. He was annoyed. He'd told her to wear her jeans and a straw hat because there would be grass burrs and hot sun. But there she sat, bare-headed, wearing shorts, miserably rubbing at her ankles.

He grunted impatiently. Annie looked up at him. "Not you," he said, stroking her fur. She patted his butt.

"Go on," Douglas said, turning his back. When he came to Therese, he said, "What's the problem?"

"No problem." She started forward without looking at him. "I was just resting."

Annie had paused to poke at something on the ground with a stick. Douglas quickened his step. Even though his students were smart, they had orangutan appetites. He always worried that they would eat something that would sicken them. "What is it?" he called.

"Dead cat," Vernon signed back. He took a picture as Annie flipped the carcass with her stick.

Therese hurried forward. "Oh, poor kitty," she said, kneeling.

Annie had seemed too absorbed in poking the cat to notice Therese approach. Only a quick eye could follow her leap. Douglas was stunned.

Both screamed. It was over.

Annie clung to Douglas's legs, whimpering.

"Shit!" Therese said. She lay on the ground, rolling from side to side, holding her left arm. Blood dripped from between her fingers.

Douglas pushed Annie back. "That was bad, *very bad*," he said. "Do you hear me?"

Annie sank down on her rump and covered her head. She hadn't gotten a child-scolding for a long time. Vernon stood beside her, shaking his head, signing, "Not wise, baboon-face."

"Stand up," Douglas said to Therese. "I can't help you right now."

Therese was pale, but dry-eyed. Clumsily, she stood and grew even paler. A hunk of flesh hung loosely from above her elbow, meaty and bleeding. "Look."

"Go on. Walk back to the house. We'll come right behind you." He tried to keep his voice calm, holding a warning hand on Annie's shoulder.

Therese moaned, catching her breath. "It hurts," she said, but stumbled on.

"We're coming," Douglas said sternly. "Just walk and—Annie, don't you dare step out of line."

They walked silently, Therese ahead, leaving drops of blood in the dirt. The drops got larger and closer together. Once, Annie dipped her finger into a bloody spot and sniffed her fingertip.

Why can't things just be easy and peaceful, he wondered? Something always happens. *Always.* He should have known better than to bring Therese around Annie. Apes didn't understand that vulnerable quality that Therese was made of. He himself didn't understand it, though at one time he'd probably been attracted to it. No—maybe he had never really seen it until it was too late. He'd only thought of Therese as "sweet" until their lives were too tangled up to keep clear of it.

Why couldn't she be as tough as Annie? Why did she always take everything so seriously?

They reached the building. Douglas sent Annie and Vernon to their rooms and guided Therese to the infirmary. He watched as Jim, their all-purpose nurse and veterinary assistant examined her arm. "I think you should probably have stitches."

He left the room to make arrangements.

Therese looked at Douglas, holding the gauze over her still-bleeding arm. "Why did she bite me?" she asked.

Douglas didn't answer. He couldn't think of how to express it.

"Do you have any idea?" she asked.

"You asked for it, all your wimping around."

"*I . . .*"

Douglas saw the anger rising in her. He didn't want to argue now. He wished he'd never brought her. He'd done it all for her, and she had ruined it.

"Don't start," he said simply, giving her a warning look.

"But, Douglas, I didn't do anything."

"Don't start," he repeated.

"I see now," she said coldly. "Somehow it's my fault again."

Jim returned with his supplies.

"Do you want me to stay?" Douglas asked. He suddenly felt a pang of guilt, realizing that she was actually hurt enough for all this attention.

"No," she said softly.

And her eyes looked far, far from him as he left her.

On the same day that the largest donation ever came to the school, a television news team came out to tape.

Douglas could tell that everyone was excited. Even the chimps that lived on the north half of the school hung on the fence and watched the TV van being unloaded. The reporter decided upon the playroom as the best location for the taping, though she didn't seem to relish sitting on the floor with the giant apes. People went over scripts, strung cords and microphones, set up hot lights, and discussed angles and sound while pointing at the high ceiling's jungle-gym design. All this to talk to a few people and an orangutan.

They brought Annie's desk into the playroom, contrary to Annie's wishes. Douglas explained that it was temporary, that these people would go away after they talked a little. Douglas and Annie stayed outside as long as possible and played Tarzan around the big tree. He tickled her. She grabbed him as he swung from a limb. "Kagoda?" she signed, squeezing him with one arm.

"Kagoda!" he shouted, laughing.

They relaxed on the grass. Douglas was hot. He felt flushed all over. "Douglas," Annie signed, "they read story?"

"Not yet. It isn't published yet."

"Why talk me?"

"Because you wrote it and sold it and people like to interview famous authors." He groomed her shoulder. "Time to go in," he said, seeing a wave from inside.

Annie picked him up in a big hug and carried him in.

"Here it is!" Douglas called to Therese, and turned on the video-recorder.

First, a long shot of the school from the dusty drive, looking only functional and square, without personality. The reporter's voice said, "Here, just south-east of town, is a special school with unusual young students. The students here have little prospect for employment when they graduate, but millions of dollars each year fund this institution."

A shot of Annie at her typewriter, picking at the keyboard with her long fingers; a sheet of paper is slowly covered with large block letters.

"This is Annie, a fifteen-year-old orangutan, who has been a student with the school for five years. She graduated with honors from another "ape school" in Georgia before coming here. And now Annie has become a writer. Recently, she sold a story to a children's magazine. The editor who bought the story didn't know that Annie was an orangutan until after she had selected the story for publication."

Annie looked at the camera uncertainly.

"Annie can read and write and understand spoken English, but she cannot speak. She uses a sign language similar to the one hearing-impaired use." Change in tone from narrative to interrogative. "Annie, how did you start writing?"

Douglas watched himself on the small screen watching Annie sign, "Teacher told me write." He saw himself grin, eyes shift slightly toward the camera, but generally watching Annie. His name and "Orangutan Teacher" appeared on the screen. The scene made him uneasy.

"What made you send in Annie's story for publication?" the reporter asked.

Douglas signed to Annie, she came to him for a hug, and turned a winsome face to the camera. "Our administrator, Dr. Morris, and I both thought it was as good as any kids' story, so Dr. Morris said, 'Send it in.' The editor liked it." Annie nervously made "pee" sign to Douglas.

Then, a shot of Dr. Morris in her office, a chimp on her lap, clapping her brown hands.

"Dr. Morris, your school was established five years ago by grants and government funding. What is your purpose here?"

"Well, in the last few decades, apes—mostly chimpanzees like Rose here—have been taught sign language experimentally. Mainly to prove that apes could indeed use language." Rosie put the tip of her finger through the gold hoop in Dr. Morris's ear. Dr. Morris took her hand away gently. "We were established with the idea of *educating* apes, a comparable education to the primary grades." She looked at the chimp. "Or however far they will advance."

"Your school has two orangutans and six chimpanzees. Are there differences in their learning?" the reporter asked.

Dr. Morris nodded emphatically. "Chimpanzees are very clever, but the orang has a different brain structure which allows for more abstract reasoning. Chimps learn many things quickly, orangs are slower. But the orangutan has the ability to learn in greater depth."

Shot of Vernon swinging on the ropes in front of the school.

Assuming that Vernon is Annie, the reporter said, "Her teacher felt from the start that Annie was an especially promising student. The basic sentences that she types out on her typewriter are simple but original entertainment."

Another shot of Annie at the typewriter.

"If you think this is just monkey business, you'd better think again. Tolstoy, watch out!"

Depressed by the lightness, brevity, and the stupid "monkey business" remark, Douglas turned off the television.

He sat for a long time. Whenever Therese had gone to bed, she had left him silently. After half an hour of staring at the blank screen, he rewound his video-recorder and ran it soundlessly until Annie's face appeared.

And then froze it. He could almost feel again the softness of her halo of red hair against his chin.

He couldn't sleep.

Therese had rumpled her way out of the sheet and lay on her side, her back to him. He looked at the shape of her shoulder and back, downward to the dip of the waist, up the curve of her hip. Her buttocks were round ovals, one atop the other. Her skin was sleek and shiny in the filtered street light coming through the window. She smelled slightly of shampoo and even more slightly of female.

What he felt for her, when he thought of her generally, anyone could call love. And yet, he found himself helplessly angry with her most of the time. When he thought he could amuse her, it would end with her feelings being hurt for some obscure reason. He heard cruel words come barging out of an otherwise gentle mouth. She took everything seriously; mishaps and misunderstandings occurred beyond his control, beyond his repair.

Under this satiny skin, she was troubled and tense. A lot of sensitivity and fear. He had stopped trying to gain access to what had been the happier parts of her person, not understanding where they had gone. He had stopped wanting to love her, but he didn't *not* want to love her, either. It just did not seem to matter.

Sometimes, he thought, it would be easier to have someone like Annie for a wife.

Annie.

He loved her furry face. He loved the unconditional joy in her face when she saw him. She was bright and warm and unafraid. She didn't read things into what he said, but listened and talked with him. They were so natural together. Annie was so filled with vitality.

Douglas withdrew his hand from Therese, whose skin seemed a bare blister of dissatisfaction.

He lay on the floor of the apes' playroom with the fan blowing across his chest. He held Annie's report on Lawrence's *Sons and Lovers* by diagonal corners to keep it from flapping.

Annie lazily swung from bars crisscrossing the ceiling.

"Paul wasn't happy at work because the boss looked over his shoulder at his handwriting," she had written. "But he was happy again later. His brother died and his mother was sad. Paul got sick. He was better and visited his friends again. His mother died and his friends didn't tickle him any more."

Douglas looked over the top of the paper at Annie. True, it was the first time she'd read an "adult" novel, but he had expected something better than this. He considered asking her if Vernon had written the report for her, but thought better of it.

"Annie," he said, sitting up. "What do you think this book is really about?"

She swung down and landed on the sofa. "About man," she said.

Douglas waited. There was no more. "But what about it? Why this man instead of another? What was special about him?"

Annie rubbed her hands together, answerless.

"What about his mother?"

"She help him," Annie answered in a flurry of dark fingers. "Especially when he paint."

Douglas frowned. He looked at the page again, disappointed.

"What I do?" Annie asked, worried.

He tried to brighten up. "You did just fine. It was a hard book."

"Annie smart," the orang signed. "Annie smart."

Douglas nodded. "I know."

Annie rose, then stood on her legs, looking like a two-story fuzzy building, teetering from side to side. "Annie smart. Writer. Smart," she signed. "Write book. Bestseller."

Douglas made a mistake. He laughed. Not as simple as a human laughing at another, this was an act of aggression. His bared teeth and uncontrolled guff-guff struck out at Annie. He tried to stop.

She made a gulping sound and galloped out of the room.

"Wait, Annie!" He chased after her.

By the time he got outside she was far ahead. He stopped running when his chest hurt and trotted slowly through the weeds toward her. She sat forlornly far away and watched him come.

When he was near, she signed "hug" three times.

Douglas collapsed, panting, his throat raw. "Annie, I'm sorry," he said. "I didn't mean it." He put his arms around her.

She held onto him.

"I love you, Annie. I love you so much I don't want ever to hurt you. Ever, ever, ever. I want to be with you all the time. Yes, you're smart and talented and good." He kissed her tough face.

Whether forgotten or forgiven, the hurt of his laughter was gone from her eyes. She held him tighter, making a soft sound in her throat, a sound for him.

They lay together in the crackling yellow weeds, clinging. Douglas felt his love physically growing for her. More passionately than ever before in his life, he wanted to make love to her. He touched her. He felt that she understood what he wanted, that her breath on his neck was anticipation. A consummation as he'd never imagined, the joining of their species in language and body. Not dumb animal-banging but mutual love . . . He climbed over her and hugged her back.

Annie went rigid when he entered her.

Slowly, she rolled away from him, but he held onto her. "No." A horrible grimace came across her face that raised the hairs on the back of Douglas's neck. "Not you," she said.

She's going to kill me, he thought.

His passion declined; Annie disentangled herself and walked away.

He sat for a moment, stunned at what he'd done, at what had happened, wondering what he would do for the rest of his life with the memory of it. Then he zipped up his pants.

Staring at his dinner plate, he thought, it's just the same as if I had been rejected by a woman.

His hands could still remember the matted feel of her fur; tucked in his groin was the memory of being in an alien place. It had made him throw up out in the field that afternoon, and afterwards he'd come straight home. He hadn't even said good night to the orangs.

"What's the matter?" Therese asked.

He shrugged.

She half-rose out of her chair to kiss him on the temple. "You don't have a fever, do you?"

"No."

"Can I do something to make you feel better?" Her hand slid along his thigh.

He stood up. "Stop it."

She sat still. "Are you in love with another woman?"

Why can't she just leave me alone. "No. I have a lot on my mind."

"It never was like this, even when you were working on your thesis."

"Therese," he said, with what he felt was undeserved patience, "just leave me alone. It doesn't help with you at me all the time."

"But I"m scared. I don't know what to do. You act like you don't want me around."

"All you do is criticize me." He stood and took his dishes to the sink.

Slowly, she trailed after him, carrying her plate. "I"m just trying to understand. It's my life, too."

He said nothing and she walked away as if someone had told her not to leave footsteps.

In the bathroom, he stripped and stood under the shower for a long time. He imagined that Annie's smell clung to him. He felt that Therese could smell it on him.

What have I done, what have I done . . . ?

And when he came out of the shower, Therese was gone.

He had considered calling in sick, but he knew that it would be just as miserable to stay around the house and think about Annie, think about Therese, and worse, to think about himself.

He dressed for work, but couldn't eat breakfast. Realizing that his pain showed, he straightened his shoulders, but found them drooping again as he got out of the car at work.

With some fear, he came through the office. The secretary greeted him with rolling eyes. "Someone's given out our number again," she said as the phone buzzed. Another line was on hold. "This morning there was a man standing at the window watching me until Gramps kicked him off the property."

Douglas shook his head in sympathy with her and approached the orang's door. He felt nauseated again.

Vernon sat at his typewriter, composing captions for his photo album. He didn't get up to greet Douglas, but gave him an evaluative stare.

Douglas patted his shoulder. "Working?" he asked.

"Like dog," Vernon said and returned to typing.

Annie sat outside on the back porch. Douglas opened the door and stood beside her. She looked up at him, but—like Vernon—made no move toward the customary hug. The morning was still cool, the shadow of the building still long in front of them. Douglas sat down.

"Annie," he said softly. "I'm sorry. I'll never do it again. You see, I felt . . . " He stopped. It wasn't any easier than it had been to talk to Oona, or Wendy, or Shelley, or Therese . . . He realized then that he didn't understand her any more than he'd understood them. Why had she rejected him? What was she thinking? What would happen from now on? Would they be friends again?

"Oh, hell," he said. He stood. "It won't happen again."

Annie gazed away into the trees.

He felt strained all over, especially in his throat. He stood by her a long time.

"I don't want write stories," she signed.

Douglas stared at her. "Why?"

"Don't want." She seemed to shrug.

Douglas wondered what had happened to the confident ape who'd planned to write a bestseller the day before. "Is that because of me?"

She didn't answer.

"I don't understand," he said. "Do you want to write it down for me? Could you explain it that way?"

"No," she signed, "can't explain. Don't want."

He continued. "What *do* you want?"

"Sit tree. Eat bananas, chocolate. Drink brandy." She looked at him seriously. "Sit tree. Day, day, day, week, month, year."

Christ almighty, he thought, she's having a goddamned existential crisis. All the years of education. All the accomplishments. The hopes of an entire field of primatology. All shot to hell because of a moody ape. It can't just be me. This would have happened sooner or later, maybe . . . He thought of all the effort he would have to make to repair their relationship. It made him tired.

"Annie, why don't we just ease up a little on your work. You can rest today. You can go sit in the trees all of today and I'll bring you a glass of wine."

She shrugged again.

Oh, I've botched it, he thought. What an idiot. He felt a pain coming back, a pain like poison, with a focal point but shooting through his heart and hands, making him dizzy and short of breath.

At least she doesn't hate me, he thought, squatting to touch her hand.

She bared her teeth.

Douglas froze. She slid away from him and headed for the trees.

• • •

He sat alone at home and watched the newscast. In a small midwestern town they burned the issues of the magazine with Annie's story in it.

A heavy woman in a windbreaker was interviewed with the bonfire in the background. "I don't want my children reading things that weren't even written by humans. I have human children and this godless ape is not going to tell its stories to them."

A quick interview with Dr. Morris, who looked even more tired and introverted than usual. "The story is a very innocent tale, told by an innocent personality. I really don't think she has any ability or intention to corrupt . . . "

He turned the television off. He picked up the phone and dialed one of Therese's friends. "Jan, have you heard from Therese yet?"

"No, sure haven't."

"Well, let me know, okay?"

"Sure."

He thought vaguely about trying to catch her at work, but he left earlier in the morning and came home later in the evening than she did.

Looking at her pictures on the wall, he thought of when they had first met, first lived together. There had been a time when he had loved her so much, he'd been bursting with it. Now he felt empty. He didn't want her to hate him, but he still didn't know if he could talk to her about what had happened. The idea that she would sit and listen to him didn't seem realistic.

Even Annie wouldn't listen to him any more.

He was alone. He'd done a big, dumb, terrible thing. It would have been different if Annie had reciprocated, if somehow they could have become lovers. Then it would have been them against the world, a new kind of relationship.

But Annie didn't seem any different to Therese when it really came down to it. She didn't have any more interest in him than Dr. Morris would have in Vemon. He'd imagined it.

He was alone. And without Annie's consent, he was just a jerk who'd fucked an ape.

"I made a mistake," he said aloud to Therese's picture. "So let's forget it."

But he couldn't forget.

"Dr. Morris wants to see you," the secretary said as he came in.

"Okay." He changed course for the administrative office. He whistled. In the past few days, Annie had been cool, but he felt that everything would settle down eventually. He felt better. Wondering what horrors or marvels Dr. Morris had to share with him, he knocked at her door and peered through the glass window. Probably another magazine burning, he thought.

She signaled him to come in. "Hello, Douglas."

Annie, he thought, *something's happened.*

He stood until she motioned him to sit down. She looked at his face for several seconds. "This is difficult for me," she said.

She's found out, he thought. But he put that aside, figuring it was a paranoia that made him worry. There's no way. No way. I have to calm down or I'll show it.

She held up a photograph.

There it was—a dispassionate and cold document of that one moment in his life. She held it up to him like an accusation. It shocked him as if it hadn't been himself,

Defiance forced him to stare at the picture instead of looking for compassion in Dr. Morris's eyes. He knew exactly where the picture had come from.

Vernon and his new telephoto lens.

He visualized the image of his act rising up in a tray of chemicals. Slowly, he looked away from it. Dr. Morris could not know how he had changed since that moment. He could make no protest or denial.

"I have no choice," Dr. Morris said flatly. "I'd always thought that even if you weren't good with people, at least you worked well with the apes. Thank God Henry, who does Vernon's darkroom work, has promised not to say anything."

Douglas was rising from his chair. He wanted to tear the picture out of her hands. He didn't want her to see it. He wanted her to ask him if he had changed, let him reassure her that it would never happen again, that he understood he'd been wrong.

But her eyes were flat and shuttered against him. "We'll send your things," she said.

He paused at his car and saw two big red shapes—one coppery orange, one chocolate-red—sitting in the trees. Vernon bellowed out a groan that ended with an alien burbling. It was a wild sound full of the jungle and steaming rain.

Douglas watched Annie scratch herself and look toward some chimps walking the land beyond their boundary fence. As she started to turn her gaze in his direction, he ducked into his car.

I guess an ape wouldn't understand me any more than a human, he thought, angrily trying to drive his shame away.

First published in *Isaac Asimov's Science Fiction Magazine,*
Mid-December, 1983.

ABOUT THE AUTHOR

Leigh Kennedy grew up in Denver and began writing in the nurturing atmosphere of the Northern Colorado Writer's Workshop. "Her Furry Face" was written during the five years she lived in Austin, Texas, before heading to England, where she's now lived for nearly thirty years. Her novels include *The Journal of Nicholas the American* and *Saint Hiroshima,* and a short-story collection, *Faces.* Her most recent book is a new collection, *Wind Angles.* She has two grown children, plays the viola socially, and writes very slowly.

Giants

PETER WATTS

So many eons, slept away while the universe wound down around him. He's dead to human eyes. Even the machines barely see the chemistry ticking over in those cells: an ancient molecule of hydrogen sulphide, frozen in a hemoglobin embrace; an electron shuttled sluggishly down some metabolic pathway two weeks ago. Back on Earth there used to be life deep in the rocks, halfway to the mantle; empires rose and fell in the time it took those microbes to draw breath. Next to Hakim's, their lives blurred past in an eyeblink. (Next to all of ours. I was every bit as dead, just a week ago.)

I'm still not sure it's a good idea, bringing him back.

Flat lines shiver in their endless march along the x-axis: molecules starting to bump against each other, core temp edging up a fraction of a fraction. A lonely spark flickers in the hypothalamus; another wriggles across the prefrontal cortex (a passing thought, millennia past its best-before, released from amber). Millivolts trickle down some random path and an eyelid twitches.

The body shudders, tries to breathe but it's too soon: it's still anoxic in there, pure H_2S gumming up the works and shutting the machinery of life down to a whisper. The Chimp starts a nitrox flush; swarms of fireflies bloom across *Pulmonary* and *Vascular*. Hakim's cold empty husk fills with light from the inside out: red and yellow isotherms, pulsing arteries, a trillion reawakening neurons stippling across the translucent avatar in my head. A real breath this time. Another. His fingers twitch and stutter, tap a random tattoo against the floor of his sarcophagus.

The lid slides open. His eyes, too, a moment later: they roll unfocused in their sockets, suffused in a haze of resurrection dementia. He can't see me. He sees soft lights and vague shadows, hears the faint underwater echo of nearby machinery, but his mind is still stuck to the past and the present hasn't sunk in yet.

A tongue dry as leather flicks into view against his upper lip. A drinking tube emerges from its burrow and nudges Hakim's cheek. His takes it in his mouth and nurses, reflexive as a newborn.

I lean into what passes for his field of view: "Lazarus, come forth."

It anchors him. I see sudden focus resolving in those eyes, see the past welling up behind them. I see memories and hearsay loading in the wake of my voice. Confusion evaporates; something sharper takes its place. Hakim stares up at me from the grave, his eyes hard as obsidian.

"You asshole," he says. "I can't believe we haven't killed you yet."

I give him space. I retreat to the forest, wander endless twilit caverns while he learns to live again. Down here I can barely see my own hand in front of my face: gray fingers, faint sapphire accents. Photophores glimmer around me like dim constellations, each tiny star lit by the glow of a trillion microbes. Photosynthesis instead of fusion. You can't get truly lost in *Eriophora*—the Chimp always knows where you are—but here in the dark, there's comfort to be had in the illusion.

Eventually, though, I have to stop stalling. I sample myriad feeds as I rise though the depths of the asteroid, find Hakim in the starboard bridge. I watch as he enters painstaking questions, processes answers, piles each new piece on top of the last in a rickety climb to insight. Lots of debris in this system, yes: more than enough material for a build. Call up the transponders and—what's this? No in-system scaffolding, no half-constructed jump gate, no asteroid mining or factory fleet. So why—?

System dynamics, now. Lagrange points. Nothing on this side, anyway, even though there are at least three planetary bodies in—whoa, those *orbits*—

Our orbit . . .

By the time I join him in the flesh he's motionless, staring into the tac tank. A bright dimensionless point floats in the center of that display: *Eriophora*. The ice giant looms dark and massive to port, the red one—orders of magnitude larger—seethes in the distance behind. (If I stepped outside I'd see an incandescent barrier stretching across half the universe, with the barest hint of a curve on the horizon; tac reduces it to a cherry globe floating in an aquarium.) A million bits of detritus, from planets to pebbles, career through the neighborhood. We're not even relativistic and still the Chimp hasn't had time to tag them all.

None of those tags make sense anyway. We're aeons from the nearest earthly constellation; every alphabet, every astronomical convention has been exhausted by the stars we've passed in the meantime. Maybe the Chimp invented his own taxonomy while we were sleeping, some arcane gibberish of hex and ASCII that makes sense to him and him alone. A hobby, perhaps, although he's supposed to be too stupid for anything like that.

I slept through most of that scenery. I've been awake for barely a hundred builds; *my* mythological reservoir is nowhere near exhausted. I have my own names for these monsters.

The cold giant is Thule. The hot one is Surtr.

Hakim ignores my arrival. He moves sliders back and forth: trajectories extrude from bodies in motion, predict the future according to Newton. Eventually all those threads converge and he rewinds time, reverses entropy, reassembles the shattered teacup and sets it running again. He does it three times as I watch. The result never changes.

He turns, his face bloodless. "We're going to hit. We're going to ram straight into the fucking thing."

I swallow and nod.

"That's how it starts," I tell him.

We're going to hit. We're *aiming* to hit, we're going to let the lesser monster devour us before the greater one devours it. We'll lower *Eriophora* by her own bootstraps, sink through roiling bands of hydrogen and helium and a thousand exotic hydrocarbons, down to whatever residual deep-space chill Thule's been hoarding since—who knows? Maybe almost as long as *we've* been in flight.

It won't last, of course. The planet's been warming ever since it started its long fall from the long dark. Its bones will survive the passage through the stellar envelope easily enough: five hours in and out, give or take. Its atmosphere won't be so lucky, though. Every step of the way Surtr's going to be stripping it down like a child licking an ice cream cone.

We'll make it through by balancing in the ever-shrinking sweet spot between a red-hot sky and the pressure cooker at Thule's core. The numbers say it'll work.

Hakim should know this already. He would have *awakened* knowing if not for that idiotic uprising of theirs. But they chose to blind themselves instead, burn out their links, cut themselves off from the very heart of the mission. So now I have to *explain* things. I have to *show* things. All that instantaneous insight we once shared, gone: one ancient fit of pique and I have to use *words*, scribble out *diagrams*, etch out painstaking codes and tokens while the clock runs down. I'd hoped that maybe, after all these red-shifted millennia, they might have reconsidered; but the look in Hakim's eyes leaves no doubt. As far as he's concerned it all happened yesterday.

I do my best. I keep the conversation strictly professional, focus on the story so far: a build, aborted. Chaos and inertia, imminent annihilation, the insane counterintuitive necessity of passing *through* a star instead of going *around* it. "What are we doing here?" Hakim asks once I've finished.

"It looked like a perfect spot." I gesture at the tank. "From a distance. Chimp even sent out the vons, but—" I shrug. "The closer we got, the worse it turned out to be."

He stares at me without speaking, so I add context: "Far as we can tell something big came through a few hundred thousand years back, knocked everything haywire. None of the planetary masses are even on the ecliptic any more. We can't find anything orbiting with an eccentricity of less than point six, there's a shitload of rogues zipping around in the halo—but by the time those numbers came back, we were already committed. So now we just buckle down through the heavy traffic, steal a gravity-assist, get back on the road."

He shakes his head. "What are we doing here?"

Oh, *that's* what he means. I tap an interface, timelapse the red giant. It jerks in the tank like a fibrillating heart. "Turns out it's an irregular variable. One complication too many, right?" Not that we'll be able thread the needle any better than the Chimp can (although of course Hakim's going to try, in these few hours left to him). But the mission has parameters. The Chimp has his algorithms. Too many unexpected variables and he wakes up the meat. That's what we're here for, after all.

That's *all* we're here for.

One more time, Hakim asks: "What are *we* doing here?"

Oh.

"You're the numbers guy," I say after a moment. "One of 'em, anyway." Out of how many thousand, stored down in the crypt?

Doesn't matter. They probably all know about me by now.

"Guess it was just your rotation," I add.

He nods. "And you? You a numbers guy too, now?"

"We come back in pairs," I say softly. "You know that."

"So it just happened to be your rotation as well."

"Look—"

"Nothing to do with your *Chimp* wanting its own personal sock-puppet on hand to keep an eye on things."

"Fuck, Hakim, what do you want me to say?" I spread my hands. "That he might want someone on deck who won't try to pull the plug the first chance they get? You think that's unreasonable, given what happened?" But he doesn't even know what happened, not first-hand. Hakim wasn't up when the mutiny went down; someone obviously told him, down through the epochs. Christ knows how much of what he heard is truth, lies, legend.

A few million years go by and suddenly I'm the bogeyman.

We fall towards ice. Ice falls towards fire. Both spill through the link and spread across the back of my skull in glorious terrifying first-person. Orders of magnitude aren't empty abstractions in here: they're life-size, you feel them in your gut. Surtr may be small to a textbook—at seven million kilometers across, it's barely big enough to get into the giant's club—but that doesn't mean shit when you meet it face to face. That's not a star out there: that's the scorching edge of all creation, that's heat-death incarnate. Its breath stinks of left-over lithium from the worlds it's *already* devoured. And the dark blemish marching across its face isn't just a *planet.* It's a melting hellscape twice the size of Uranus, it's frozen methane and liquid hydrogen and a core hot and heavy enough to bake diamonds. Already it's coming apart before my eyes, any moons long since lost, the tattered remnants of a ring system shredding around it like a rotting halo. Storms boil across its face; aurorae flicker madly at both poles. A supercyclone pinwheels at the center of the dark side, fed by turbulent streamers fleeing from light into shadow. Its stares back at me like the eye of a blind god.

Meanwhile, Hakim pushes balls around inside an aquarium.

He's been at it for hours: a bright blue marble here, a sullen red basketball over there, threads of tinsel looping through time and trajectory like the webbing of some crazed spacefaring spider. Maybe pull our center of mass to starboard, start gentle then ramp up to max? Break some rocks on the way, suffer some structural damage but nothing the drones won't be able to patch up in time for the next build.

No?

Maybe cut smooth and fast into full reverse. *Eri*'s not built for it but if we keep the vectors dead along the centerline, no turn no torque just a straight linear one-eighty back out the way we came—

But no.

If only we hadn't already fallen so far down the well. If only we hadn't slowed down to open the trunk, all these N-bodies wouldn't have been able to get such a grip on us. But now we're only fast, not fast enough;

we're big but still too small.

Now, the only way out is through.

Hakim's not an idiot. He knows the rules as well as I do. He keeps trying, though. He'd rather rewrite the laws of physics than trust himself to the enemy. We'll be deaf and blind in there, after all; the convulsions of Thule's disintegrating atmosphere will fog our sight at short range, the roar of Surtr's magnetic field will deafen us in the long. There'll be no way of telling where we are, nothing but the Chimp's math to tell us where we should be.

Hakim doesn't see the world like I do. He doesn't like having to take things on faith.

Now he's getting desperate, blasting chunks off his toy asteroid in an attempt to reduce its momentum. He hasn't yet considered how that might impact our radiation shielding once we get back up to speed. He's still stuck on whether we can scavenge enough in-system debris to patch the holes on our way out.

"It won't work," I tell him, though I'm wandering deep in the catacombs half a kilometer from his location. (I'm not spying because he knows I'm watching. Of course he knows.)

"Won't it now."

"Not enough mass along the escape trajectory, even if the vons *could* grab it all and get it back in time."

"We don't know how much mass is out there. Haven't plotted it all yet."

He's being deliberately obtuse, but I go along with it; at least we're talking. "Come on. You don't need to plot every piece of gravel to get a mass distribution. It won't work. Check with the Chimp if you don't believe me. He'll tell you."

"It just *has* told me," he says.

I stop walking. I force myself to take a slow breath.

"I'm *linked,* Hakim. Not possessed. It's just an interface."

"It's a corpus callosum."

"I'm just as autonomous as you are."

"Define *I.*"

"I don't—"

"Minds are holograms. Split one in half, you get two. Stitch two together, you get one. Maybe you were human back before your *upgrade.* Right now you've got about as much standalone soul as my parietal lobe."

I look back along the vaulted corridor (I suppose the cathedral architecture might just be coincidence), where the dead sleep stacked on all sides.

They're much better company like this.

"If that's true," I ask them all, "then how did *you* ever get free?"

Hakim doesn't speak for a moment.

"The day you figure that out," he says, "is the day we lose the war."

It's not a war. It's a fucking tantrum. They tried to derail the mission and the Chimp stopped them. Simple as that, and perfectly predictable. That's why the engineers made the Chimp so minimalist in the first place, why the mission isn't run by some transcendent AI with an eight-dimensional IQ: so that things will *stay* predictable. If my fellow meat sacks couldn't see it coming, they're more stupid than the thing they're fighting.

Hakim knows that on some level, of course. He just refuses to believe it: that he and his buddies got outsmarted by something with half his synapse count. *The Chimp*. The idiot savant, the artificial stupidity. The number-cruncher explicitly designed to be so dim that even with half the lifespan of a universe to play around in, it could never develop its own agenda.

They just can't believe it beat them in a fair fight.

That's why they need me. I let them tell each other that it cheated. No way that glorified finger-counter would've won if I hadn't betrayed my own kind.

This is the nature of my betrayal; I stepped in to save their lives. Not that their lives were really in danger, of course, no matter what they say. It was just a strategy. That was predictable too.

I'm sure the Chimp would have turned the air back on before things went too far.

Thule's graduated from world to wall while I wasn't looking: a dark churning expanse of thunderheads and planet-shredding tornadoes. There's no sign of Surtr lurking behind, not so much as a faint glow on the horizon. We huddle in the shadow of the lesser giant and it's almost as though the greater one has simply gone away.

We're technically in the atmosphere now, a mountain wallowing high above the clouds with its nose to the stars. You could draw a line from the hot hydrogen slush of Thule's core through the cold small singularity of our own, straight out through the gaping conical maw at our bow. Hakim does just that, in the tac tank. Maybe it makes him feel a little more in control.

Eriophora sticks out her tongue.

You can only see it in X-ray or Hawking, maybe the slightest nimbus of gamma radiation if you tune the sensors just right. A tiny bridge opens at the back of *Eri*'s mouth: a hole in spacetime reaching back to the hole in our heart. Our center of mass smears a little off-center, seeks some elastic equilibrium between those points. The Chimp nudges the far point farther and our center follows in its wake. The asteroid tugs upward, falling after itself; Thule pulls us back. We hang balanced in the sky while the wormhole's tip edges past the crust, past that abraded mouth of blue-sanded basalt, out past the forward sensor hoop.

We've never stretched ourselves so thin before. Usually there's no need; with lightyears and epochs to play in, even the slowest fall brings us up to speed in plenty of time. We can't go past twenty percent lightspeed anyway, not without getting cooked by the blueshift. Usually *Eri* keeps her tongue in her mouth.

Not this time. This time we're just another one of Hakim's holiday ornaments, dangling from a thread in a hurricane. According to the Chimp, that thread should hold. There are error bars, though, and not a lot of empirical observation to hang them on. The database on singularities nested inside asteroids nested inside incinerating ice giants is pretty heavy on the handwaving.

And that's just the problem *within* the problem. Atmospheric docking with a world falling at two hundred kilometers a second is downright trivial next to predicting Thule's course inside the star: the drag inflicted by a millionth of a red-hot gram per cubic centimeter, stellar winds and thermohaline mixing, the deep magnetic torque of fossil helium. It's tough enough figuring out what "inside" even *means* when the gradient from vacuum to degenerate matter blurs across three million kilometers. Depending on your definition we might already be in the damn thing.

Hakim turns to me as the Chimp lowers us toward the storm. "Maybe we should wake them up."

"Who?"

"Sunday. Ishmael. All of them."

"You know how many thousands of us are stacked up down there?" *I* know. Hakim might guess but this traitor knows right down to the last soul, without checking.

Not that any of them would pat me on the back for that.

"What for?" I ask.

He shrugs. "It's all theory. You know that. We could all be dead in a day."

"You want to bring them back so they can be awake when they die?"

"So they can—I don't know. Write a poem. Grow a sculpture. Shit, one or two of them might even be willing to make their peace with *you* before the end."

"Say we wake them up and we're *not* all dead in day. You've just pushed our life support three orders of mag past spec."

He rolls his eyes. "Then we put everyone back down again. So it spikes the CO_2. Nothing the forest won't be able to clear in a few centuries."

I can barely hear the tremor in his voice.

He's scared. That's what this is. He's scared, and he doesn't want to die alone. And I don't count.

I suppose it's a start.

"Come on. At the very least it'll be a hell of a solstice party."

"Ask the Chimp," I suggest.

His face goes hard. I keep mine blank.

I'm pretty sure he wasn't serious anyway.

The depths of the troposphere. The heart of the storm. Cliffs of water and ammonia billow across our path: airborne oceans shattered down to droplets, to crystals. They crash into our mountain at the speed of sound, freeze solid or cascade into space depending on the mood. Lightning flashes everywhere, stamps my brain stem with half-glimpsed afterimages: demon faces, and great clawed hands with too many fingers.

Somehow the deck stays solid beneath my feet, unmoved even by the death throes of a world. I can't entirely suppress my own incredulity; even anchored by two million tonnes of basalt and a black hole, it seems impossible that we're not being tossed around like a mote in a wind tunnel.

I squash the feed and the carnage vanishes, leaving nothing behind but bots and bulkheads and a ribbon of transparent quartz looking down onto the factory floor. I kill some time watching the assembly lines boot up in there, watching maintenance drones gestate in the vacuum past the viewport. Even best-case there's going to be damage. Cameras blinded by needles of supersonic ice or sheets of boiling acid. The whiskers of long-range antennae, drooping in the heat. Depending on the breaks it could take an army to repair the damage after we complete our passage. I take some comfort from the sight of the Chimp's troops assembling themselves.

For an instant I think I hear a faint shriek down some far-off corridor: a breach, a decompression? No alarms, though. Probably just one of the roaches skidding around a bend in the corridor, looking for a recharge.

I'm not imagining the beeping in my head, though: Hakim, calling down from the bridge. "You need to be up here," he says when I open the channel.

"I'm on the other side of the—"

"*Please,*" he says, and forks me a live feed: one of the bow clusters, pointing at the sky.

A feature has emerged from the featureless overcast: a bright dimple on the dark sky, like a finger poking down through the roof of the world. It's invisible in visible light, hidden by torrents of ammonia and hydrocarbon hurricanes: but it shimmers in infrared like a rippling ember.

I have no idea what it is.

I draw an imaginary line through the ends of the wormhole. "It's in line with our displacement vector."

"No *shit* it's in line. I think the wormhole's—provoking it, somehow."

It's radiating at over two thousand Kelvin.

"So we're inside the star," I say, and hope Hakim takes it as good news. If nothing else, it means we're on schedule.

We've got so little to go on. We don't know how far we are from the ceiling: it keeps ablating away above us. We don't know how close we are to the core: it keeps swelling beneath the easing weight of all this shedding atmosphere. All we know is that temperature rises overhead and we descend; pressure rises from beneath and we climb. We're specks in the belly of some fish in empty mid-ocean, surface and seabed equally hypothetical. None of our reference points are any more fixed than we are. The Chimp presents estimates based on gravity and inertia, but even those are little more than guesses thanks to wormhole corruption of the local spacetime. We're stretched across the probability wave, waiting for the box to open so the universe can observe whether we're dead or alive.

Hakim eyes me from across the tank, his face flickering in the light of a hundred cam feeds. "Something's wrong. We should be through by now."

He's been saying that for the past hour.

"There's bound to be variability," I remind him. "The model—"

"The model." He manages a short, bitter laugh. "Based on all those zettabytes we collected the *other* times we hitched a ride through a red giant. The model's shit. One hiccup in the magnetic field and we could be going *down* instead of *out.*"

"We're still here."

"That's exactly the problem."

"It's still dark." The atmosphere's still thick enough to keep Surtr's blinding interior at bay.

"Always darkest before the dawn," Hakim says grimly, and points to that brightening smudge of infrared overhead.

The Chimp can't explain it, for all the fresh realtime data he stuffs into his equations. All we know is that whatever it is, it hasn't budged from our displacement vector and it's getting hotter. Or maybe closer. It's hard to tell; our senses are hazy that far out, and we're not about to stick our heads above the clouds for a better view.

Whatever it is, the Chimp doesn't think it's worth worrying about. He says we're almost through.

The storm no longer freezes on impact. It spits and hisses, turns instantly to steam. Incessant lightning strobes the sky, stop-animates towering jigsaw monsters of methane and acetylene.

God's mind might look like this, if He were an epileptic.

We get in the way sometimes, block some deific synapse in mid-discharge: a million volts spike the hull and a patch of basalt turns to slag, or *Eri* goes blind in another eye. I've lost count of the cameras and antennae and radar dishes we've already lost. I just add it to the tally when another facet flares and goes dark at the edge of the collage.

Hakim doesn't. "Play that again," he tells the Chimp. "That feed. Just before it fratzed."

The last moments of the latest casualty: *Eri's* cratered skin, outcroppings of half-buried machinery. Lightning flickers in from Stage Left, stabs a radiator fin halfway to our lumpy horizon. A flash. A banal and overfamiliar phrase:

No Signal.

"Again," Hakim says. "The strike in the middle distance. Freeze on that."

Three bolts, caught in the act—and Hakim's onto something, I see now. There's something different about them, something less—random— than the fractal bifurcations of more distant lightning. Different color, too—more of a bluish edge—and smaller. The bolts in the distance are massive. These things arcing across the crust don't look much thicker than my own arm.

They converge towards some bright mass just barely out of camera range.

"Static discharge of some kind," I suggest.

"Yeah? What *kind*, exactly?"

I can't see anything similar in the current mosaic, but the bridge bulkheads only hold so many windows and our surface cams still number in the thousands. Even my link can't handle that many feeds at once. "Chimp: any other phenomena like that on the surface?"

"Yes," says the Chimp, and high-grades the display:

Bright meshes swarming over stone and steel. Formations of ball lightning, *walking* on jagged stilts of electricity. Some kind of flat flickering plasma, sliding along *Eri*'s crust like a stingray.

"*Shittttt . . .*" Hakim hisses. "Where did *they* come from?"

Our compound eye loses another facet.

"They're targeting the sensors." Hakim's face is ashen.

"They?" Could just be electricity arcing to alloy.

"They're blinding us. Oh Jesus fuck being trapped inside a star isn't bad enough there's gotta be *hostile aliens* in the bargain."

My eyes flicker to the ceiling pickup. "Chimp, what *are* those things?"

"I don't know. They could be something like Saint Elmo's Fire, or a buoyant plasma. I can't rule out some sort of maser effect either, but I'm not detecting any significant microwave emissions."

Another camera goes down. "Lightning bugs," Hakim says, and emits a hysterical giggle.

"Are they alive?" I wonder.

"Not organically," the Chimp tells me. "I don't know if they'd meet definitions based on entropy restriction."

No conventional morphology there. Those aren't legs exactly, they're—transient voltage arcs of some kind. And body shape—if *body* even applies—seems to be optional and fluid. Auroras bunch up into sparking balls; balls sprout loops or limbs or just blow away at Mach 2, vanishing into the storm.

I call up a tactical composite. Huh: clustered distribution. A flock gathered at the skeletal remains of a long-dead thruster nozzle; another flickering across an evagineering hutch halfway down the starboard lateral line. A whole party in *Eri*'s crater-mouth, swarming around our invisible bootstrap like water circling a drain.

"Holes," Hakim says softly. "Depressions. Hatches."

But something's caught my eye that doesn't involve any of those things, something unfolding overhead while our other eyes are fixed on the ground—

"They're trying to get in. That's what they're doing."

A sudden bright smudge in the sky. Then a tear; a hole; the dilating pupil of some great demonic eye. Dim bloody light floods down across the battered landscape as a cyclone opens over our heads, wreathed in an inflammation of lightning.

Surtr's finger stretches down from Hades, visible at last to naked eyes.

"Holy *shit . . .*" Hakim whispers.

It's an incandescent tornado, a pillar of fire. It's outside reaching in, and if anything short of magic can explain its existence it's not known to me or the Chimp or the accumulated wisdom of all the astrophysicists nesting in our archives. It reaches down and touches our wormhole, just *so*. It *bulges,* as if inflamed by an embedded splinter; the swollen tip wobbles absurdly for a moment, then bursts—

—and fire gushes down from the heavens in a liquid cascade. The things beneath scatter fast as forked lightning can carry them; here in the bridge, the view sparks and dies. From a dozen other viewpoints I see tongues of soft red plasma splashing across *Eriophora*'s crust.

Some rough alarm whispers *fuck fuck fuck fuck* at my side while *Eri* feeds me intelligence: something happening back at that lateral hutch. All those cams are down but there's a pressure surge at the outer hatch and a rhythmic hissing sound crackles in along the intercom.

Hakim's vanished from the bridge. I hear the soft whine of his roach receding at full throttle. I duck out into the corridor, grab my own roach from its socket, follow. There's really no question where he's headed; I'd know that even if the Chimp hadn't already laid out the map in my head.

Way back along our starboard flank, something's knocking on the door.

He's in the prep compartment by the time I catch up, scrambling into an EVA suit like some panicky insect trying to climb back into its cocoon. "Outer hatch is breached," he tells me, forgetting.

Just meters away. Past racks and suit alcoves, just the other side of that massive biosteel drawbridge, something's looking for a way in. It could find one, too; I can see heat shimmering off the hatch. I can hear the pop and crackle of arcing electricity coming through from the other side, the faint howl of distant hurricanes.

"No weapons." Hakim fumbles with his gauntlets. "Mission to the end of time and *they don't even give us weapons.*" Which is not entirely true. They certainly gave us the means to *build* weapons. I don't know if Hakim ever availed himself of that option but I remember his buddies, not so far from this very spot. I remember them pointing their weapons at me.

"What are we doing here?" I gesture at the hatch; is it my imagination, or has it brightened a little in the center?

He shakes his head, his breathing fast and shallow. "I was gonna—you know, the welding torches. The lasers. Thought we could stand them off."

All stored on the other side.

He's suited up to the neck. His helmet hangs on its hook within easy reach: a grab and a twist and he'll be self-contained again. For a while.

Something pounds hard on the hatch. "Oh shit," Hakim says weakly.

I keep my voice level. "What's the plan?"

He takes a breath, steadies himself. "We, um—we retreat. Out past the nearest dropgate." The Chimp takes the hint and throws an overlay across my inner map; back into the corridor and fifteen meters forward. "Anything breaches, the gates come down." He nods at an alcove. "Grab a suit, just in—"

"And when they breach the dropgates?" I wonder. The biosteel's definitely glowing, there in the center.

"The *next* set goes down. Jesus, you know the drill."

"That's your plan? Give up *Eri* in stages?"

"Small stages." He nods and swallows. "Buy time. Figure out their weak spot." He grabs his helmet and turns towards the corridor.

I lay a restraining hand on his shoulder. "How do we do that, exactly?"

He shrugs it off. "Wing it for fucksake! Get Chimp to customize some drones to go in and, and ground them or something." He heads for the door.

This time the hand I lay on him is more than a suggestion. This time it clamps down, spins him around, pushes him against the bulkhead. His helmet bounces across the deck. His clumsy gloved hands come up to fend me off but there's no strength in them. His eyes do a mad little jig in his face.

"You're not thinking this through," I say, very calmly.

"*There's no time to think it through!* They might not even *get* past the gates, maybe they're not even *trying*, I mean—" His eyes brighten with faint and ridiculous hope. "Maybe it's not even an attack, I bet it's not, you know, they're just—they're *dying*. It's the end of the world and their home's on fire and they're just looking for a place to hide, they're not looking for a way *in* they're looking for a way *out*—"

"What makes you think that inside's any less lethal to them than outside is to us?"

"They don't have to be smart!" he cries out. "They just have to be scared!"

Fingers of faint electricity flicker and crackle around the edges of the hatch: heat lightning, maybe. Or maybe something more prehensile.

I keep Hakim pinned. "What if they *are* smart? What if they're not just burrowing on instinct? What if *they're* the ones with the plan, hmm?"

He spreads his hands. "What else can we do?"

"We don't give them the chance to breach. We get out of here *now*."

"Get—"

"Ditch the ice giant. Take our chances in the star."

He stops struggling and stares, waiting for the punchline. "You're insane," he whispers when I fail to deliver.

"Why? Chimp says we're almost through anyway."

"He said that *half an hour ago!* And we were an hour past predicted exit even *then!*"

"Chimp?" I say, not for the AI's benefit but for Hakim's.

"Right here."

"Say we max the wormhole. Throw out as much mass as we can, shortest path out of the envelope."

"Tidal stress tears *Eriophora* into two debris clouds of roughly equal mass, each one centered on—"

"Amend that. Say we optimize distance and displacement to maximize velocity *without* losing structural integrity."

I can tell by the wait that there are going to be serious confidence limits attached to the answer. "*Eriophora* is directly exposed to the stellar envelope for 1300 corsecs," he says at last. "Give or take 450."

At 2300 Kelvin. Basalt melts at 1724.

But the Chimp hasn't finished. "We would also risk significant structural damage due to the migration of secondary centers-of-mass beyond *Eriophora's* hardlined displacement channels."

"Do we make it?"

"I don't know."

Hakim throws up his hands. "Why the hell not? It's what you *do!*"

"My models can't account for the plasma invagination overhead or the electrical events on the hull," the Chimp tells him. "Therefore they're missing at least one important variable. You can't trust my predictions."

Down at the end of the compartment, the hatch glows red as the sky. Electricity sizzles and pops and *grabs.*

"Do it," Hakim says suddenly.

"I need consensus," the Chimp replies.

Of course. The Chimp takes his lead from us meat sacks when he gets lost; but looking to us for wisdom, he wouldn't know whose to follow if we disagreed.

Hakim waits, manic, his eyes flicking between me and the hatch. "Well?" he says after a moment.

It all comes down to me. I could cancel him out.

"What are you waiting for? *It was your fucking idea!*"

I feel an urge to lean close and whisper in his ear. *Not just Chimp's sock puppet now, am I, motherfucker?* I resist it. "Sure," I say instead. "Give it a shot."

Wheels begin to turn. *Eriophora* trembles and groans, torqued by vectors she was never designed for. Unfamiliar sensations tickle my backbrain, move forward, root in my gut: the impossible, indescribable sense of *down* being in two places at once. One of those places is safe and familiar, beneath my feet, beneath decks and forests and bedrock at the very heart of the ship; but the other's getting stronger, and it's *moving*...

I hear the scream of distant metal. I hear the clatter of loose objects crashing into walls. *Eriophora* lurches, staggers to port, turns ponderously on some axis spread across too many sickening dimensions. There's something moving behind the wall, deep in the rocks; I can't see it but I feel its pull, hear the cracking of new fault lines splitting ancient stone. A dozen crimson icons bloom like tumors in my brain, *Subsystem Failure* and *Critical Coolant* and *Primary Channel Interrupt*. A half-empty squeezebulb, discarded decades or centuries or millennia ago, wobbles half-levitating into view around the corner. It falls sideways and slides along the bulkhead, caught up in the tide-monster's wake.

I'm standing on the deck at forty-five degrees. I think I'm going to be sick.

The *down* beneath my feet is less than a whisper. I give silent thanks for superconducting ceramics, piezoelectric trusses, all reinforcements brute and magical that keep this little worldlet from crumbling to dust while the Chimp plays havoc with the laws of physics. I offer a diffuse and desperate prayer that they're up to the task. Then I'm falling forward, upward, *out*: Hakim and I smack into the forward bulkhead as a rubber band, stretched to its limit, snaps free and hurls us forward.

Surtr roars in triumph as we emerge, snatches at this tiny unexpected prize shaken free of the larger one. Jagged spiders leap away and vanish into blinding fog. Wireframe swirls of magnetic force twist in the heat, spun off from the dynamo way down in the giant's helium heart—or maybe that's just the Chimp, feeding me models and imaginings. I'm pretty sure it's not real; our eyes and ears and fingertips have all been licked away, our windows all gone dark. Skin and bones will be next to go: warm basalt, softening down to plastic. Maybe it's happening already. No way to tell any more. Nothing to do but fall out as the air flattens and shimmers in the rising heat.

I'm saving your life, Hakim. You better fucking appreciate it.

Yeats was wrong. The center held after all.

Now we are only half-blind, and wholly ballistic. A few eyes remain smoldering on the hull, pitted with cataracts; most are gone entirely.

Charred stumps spark fitfully where sensors used to be. *Eri*'s center of mass has snapped back into itself and is sleeping off the hangover down in the basement. We coast on pure inertia, as passive as any other rock.

But we are through, and we are alive, and we have ten thousand years to lick our wounds.

It won't take anywhere near that long, of course. The Chimp has already deployed his army; they burned their way out through the slagged doorways of a dozen service tunnels, laden with newly refined metals dug from the heart of the mountain. Now they clamber across the surface like great metal insects, swapping good parts for bad and cauterizing our wounds with bright light. Every now and then another dead window flickers back to life; the universe returns to us in bits and pieces. Surtr simmers in our wake, still vast but receding, barely hot enough to boil water this far out.

I prefer the view ahead: deep comforting darkness, swirls of stars, glittering constellations we'll never see again and can't be bothered to name. Just passing through.

Hakim should be down in the crypt by now, getting ready to turn in. Instead I find him back in the starboard bridge, watching fingers of blue-white lightning leap across the hull. It's a short clip and it always ends the same way, but he seems to find value in repeat viewings.

He turns at my approach. "Sanduloviciu plasma."

"What?"

"Electrons on the outside, positive ions on the inside. Self-organizing membranes. Live ball lightning. Although I don't know what they'd use as a rep code. Some kind of quantum spin liquid, maybe." He shrugs. "The guys who discovered these things didn't have much to say about heredity."

He's talking about primitive experiments with gas and electricity, back in some prehistoric lab from the days before we launched (I know: Chimp fed me the archive file the moment Hakim accessed it). "*We're* the guys who discovered them," I point out; the things that clawed at our doorstep were lightyears beyond anything those cavemen ever put together.

"No we didn't."

I wait.

"*They* discovered *us,*" he tells me.

I feel a half-smile pulling at the corner of my mouth.

"I keep thinking about the odds," Hakim says. "A system that looks so right from a distance and turns out to be so wrong after we've committed to the flyby. All that mass and all those potential trajectories, and somehow the only way out is through the goddamn star. Oh, and there's one convenient ice giant that just *happens* to be going our way. Any idea what those odds are?"

"Astronomical." I keep a straight face.

He shakes his head. "Infinitesimal."

"I've been thinking the same thing," I admit.

Hakim gives me a sharp glance. "Have you now."

"The way the whole system seemed primed to draw us into the star. The way that thing reached down to grab us once we were inside. Your *lightning bugs*: I don't think they were native to the planet at all, not if they were plasma-based."

"You think they were from the star."

I shrug.

"Star aliens," Hakim says.

"Or drones of some kind. Either way, you're right; this system didn't just happen. It was a sampling transect. A trapline."

"Which makes us what, exactly? Specimens? Pets? Hunting trophies?"

"Almost. Maybe. Who knows?"

"Maybe *buddies,* hmm?"

I glance up at the sudden edge in his voice.

"Maybe just *allies,*" he muses. "In adversity. Because it's all for one against the common enemy, right?"

"That's generally good strategy." It felt good, too, not being the bad guy for a change. Being the guy who actually pulled asses *out* of the fire. I'll settle for *allies.*

"Because I can see a couple of other coincidences, if I squint." He's not squinting, though. He's staring straight through me. "Like the way the Chimp happened to pair me up with the one person on the whole roster I'd just as soon chuck out an airlock."

"That's hardly a coincidence," I snort. "It'd be next to impossible to find someone who *didn't*—"

Oh.

The accusation hangs in the air like static electricity. Hakim waits for my defense.

"You think the Chimp used this situation to—"

"Used," he says, "or *invented.*"

"That's insane. You saw it with your own eyes, you can *still* see—"

"I saw models in a tank. I saw pixels on bulkheads. I never threw on a suit to go see for myself. You'd have to be suicidal, right?"

He's actually smiling.

"They tried to break in," I remind him.

"Oh, I know *something* was pounding on the door. I'm just not sold on the idea that it was built by aliens."

"You think this whole thing was some kind of trick?" I shake my head in disbelief. "We'll have surface access in a couple of weeks. Hell, just cut a hole into Fab right now, crawl out through one of the service tunnels. See for yourself."

"See what? A star off the stern?" He shrugs. "Red giants are common as dirt. Doesn't mean the specs on this system were anywhere near as restrictive as Chimp says. Doesn't mean we had to go *through,* doesn't even mean we did. For all I know the Chimp had its bots strafing the hull with lasers and blowtorches for the past hundred years, slagging things down to look nice and convincing just in case I *did* pop out for a look-see." Hakim shakes his head. "All I know is, it's only had one meat sack in its corner since the mutiny, and he's not much good if no one will talk to him. But how can you keep hating someone after he's saved your life?"

It astonishes me, the degree to which people torture reason. Just to protect their precious preconceptions.

"The weird thing," Hakim adds, almost to himself, "is that it worked."

It takes a moment for that to sink in.

"Because I don't think you were in on it," he explains. "I don't think you had a clue. How could you? You're not even a whole person, you're just a—a glorified subroutine. And subroutines don't question their inputs. A thought pops into your head, you just assume it's yours. You believe everything that miserable piece of hardware tells you, because you don't have a choice. Maybe you never did.

"How can I hate you for that?" he asks.

I don't answer, so he does: "I can't. Not any more. I can only—"

"Shut the fuck up," I say, and turn my back.

He leaves me then, leaves me surrounded by all these pixels and pictures he refuses to accept. He heads back to the crypt to join his friends. The sleeping dead. The weak links. Every last one of them would scuttle the mission, given half a chance.

If it was up to me none of them would ever wake up again. But Chimp reminds me of the obvious: a mission built for aeons, the impossibility of anticipating even a fraction of the obstacles we're bound to encounter. The need for flexibility, for the wet sloppy intelligence that long-dead engineers excluded from his architecture in the name of mission stability. Billions of years ahead of us, perhaps, and only a few thousand meat sacks to deal with the unexpected. There may not be enough of us as it is.

And yet, with all that vaunted human intellect, Hakim can't see the obvious. None of them can. I'm not even human to those humans. A subroutine, he says. A lobe in something else's brain. But I don't need his fucking pity. He'd realize that if he thought about it for more than a split-second, if he was willing to examine that mountain of unexamined assumptions he calls a worldview.

He won't, though. He refuses to look into the mirror long enough to see what's looking back. He can't even tell the difference between brain and brawn. The Chimp drives the ship; the Chimp builds the jump gates; the Chimp runs life support. We try to take the reins of our own destiny and it's the Chimp who hammers us down.

So the Chimp is in control. The Chimp is always in control; and when minds merge across this high-bandwidth link in my head, surely it will be the mech that absorbs the meat.

It astonishes me that he can't see the fallacy. He knows the Chimp's synapse count as well as I do, but he'd rather fall back on prejudice than run the numbers.

I'm not the Chimp's subroutine at all.

The Chimp is mine.

First published in *Extreme Planets*,
edited by David Conyers, David Kernot, and Jeff Harris, 2014.

ABOUT THE AUTHOR

Peter Watts–author of *Blindsight, Echopraxia,* and the Rifters Trilogy, among other things–seems especially popular among people who dont know him. At least, he wins most of his awards overseas except for a Hugo (won thanks to fan outrage over an altercation with Homeland Security) a Jackson (won thanks to fan sympathy over nearly dying from flesh-eating disease), and a couple of dick-ass Canadian awards you've probably never heard of. *Blindsight* is a core text for university courses ranging from Philosophy to Neuropsychology, despite an unhealthy focus on space vampires. Watts's work is available in eighteen languages.

Flash Gordon, Cardboard Space Stations, and Zero Gravity Sex: Why Science Fiction Isn't Always to Blame
MARK COLE

It was early July of 1960 and Flash Gordon was in trouble.

A deadly virus had Flash, Dale and Doctor Zarkov trapped on a space station as it killed one crewmember after another. However, on July 12, Zarkov and the team of doctors discovered the answer:

Interferon.

For most people watching the victims' rapid recovery, it was the first time they'd ever heard of the new miracle drug, which Alick Isaacs had discovered only three years before. However, it wouldn't be the last: experts hailed it as "penicillin for viruses" and promised that it would cure the common cold and wipe out nearly every viral infection.

But it didn't quite work out that way.

The discovery of interferon was one of those moments which beautifully illustrates how sudden intuitive insights spark new discoveries. At the time, biologists believed that the cell had no means of fighting a viral attack. If this attack slowed, it was because of some external factor—bits of the virus stuck in the cell membrane, perhaps—or the virus had exhausted the cell's resources. Isaacs began to suspect, however, that there had to be something attacking the virus. He devised a simple but elegant experiment using fertile hen's eggs and discovered a mysterious protein which "interfered" with the action of the virus.

However, many of his fellow virologists sneered at his discovery (one of them dubbing it "misinterpreton"), claiming that his results were the result of a laboratory error. Isaacs began to believe he had accidentally contaminated his experiment, became depressed and was briefly institutionalized—and then someone else repeated his results.

The possibilities of such a discovery were obvious, and once it was accepted, the wild claims about interferon soon started. The problem was that Isaacs just didn't have the methods he needed to isolate and study the elusive protein. Isaacs spent the rest of his life on his research (he died less than a decade later at age forty-five) but never got to see it come to fruition.

We now know that there are ten different interferons (seven in our cells). They've been used to treat a wide range of illnesses from genital warts, to tumors, certain viral infections and MPN (blood cancer).

But we still don't have the interferon nasal spray—the instant cure for the common cold—which *Omni* magazine confidently predicted in 1982 would be in every medicine cabinet by the end of the decade. It is actually available in Russia and parts of Europe, but it causes bleeding in ten percent of those who use it—and most experts do not believe that the doses are anywhere near high enough to work.

There is no question that interferon is an absolutely incredible breakthrough. It just doesn't do everything people hoped it would.

Science and science fiction have long had an uncomfortable relationship.

At times it seems like they just can't stay together. Writers who strove mightily to keep their books accurate are today often held up to scorn. Their problem far too often was that the real discoveries and scientific ideas at the heart of their work ended up exaggerated almost beyond recognition.

Science fiction gets blamed most of the time. After all, we all know that fiction is a work of imagination. But far too often—and despite all the familiar claims of scientific objectivity—it has been scientists who allow their imaginations to get caught up in visions of the incredible new future their efforts will bring about.

One of the worst "offenders" was Willy Ley.

His book, *The Conquest of Space,* ranks as one of the most successful works of popular science ever. Millions read its dazzling predictions of the step-by-step program which would take us into space. We would live there, work there, study the universe there, then move on past our world to explore others. Equally stunning were the illustrations by the great Chesley Bonestell, who gave incredible solidity and believability to Willy's most extravagant claims.

Even more extravagant was the series of children's books the two produced, with titles like *Space Station* and *Space Pilots* (my ragged third-hand copies were among my greatest childhood treasures). Chesley's stunning art takes over, in full color and often full page; full of incredible vehicles, men working in space, detailed views of the station and life inside it. The two were a true dream team, bringing their vision to life with a flair few science fiction writers of the age managed.

Naturally, their work inspired a lot of science fiction: many writers borrowed heavily from Ley's vision of life in space, and Bonestell's art occasionally graced their stories. In the movies, Chesley created mattes and vehicle designs for *Destination Moon, When Worlds Collide,* and *It! The Terror from Beyond Space.* Perhaps his finest moment was his work for the movie "adaptation" of *The Conquest of Space,* which includes a space station and a winged Mars lander. It's almost enough to make us ignore the grizzled, hard-headed military scientist leading the expedition suddenly developing religious mania.

Almost.

Even those films Bonestell didn't actually design often steal from him, with Hammer's *Spaceways, The Green Slime* and Antonio Margheriti's Spaghetti space operas among the most shameless. His wheel-shaped space stations have become a cultural icon, making appearances in everything from *Doctor Who* to Toho's giant asteroid film, *Gorath. Robot Bastard!* even features one made out of corrugated cardboard.

Behind all Ley's predictions lay all the years he'd spent researching rocketry, first for the Germans, then for our space program. His research informed all the colorful Bonestell illustrations, and his books never shied away from discussing the hard science backing up his predictions. It was, in fact, a brilliant piece of work.

Which doesn't mean he didn't get things wrong.

Or even very wrong.

Politics drove some of the biggest departures from Ley's predictions. The X-15 was always meant to be a precursor to Ley's reusable space planes (a few years ago we reclassified its pilots as astronauts). However, the X-15B, a radical re-engineering of the plane that would have made it the next best thing to a space ship, got cancelled when our space program's goal became putting a man in space as soon as possible, even if it meant sticking him in a tin can with an oversized firecracker under it.

But when NASA finally returned to his dream of reusable space planes, with soaring promises of space stations and Mars expeditions, it didn't work out as predicted.

One of his most visible mistakes is also the one that few people notice: He portrayed his astronauts putting the big wheel together piece by piece, welding girders and panels together in space (an image which makes a brief onscreen appearance in *2001: A Space Odyssey*)

However, when we built the ISS, we sent up individual pre-fab modules, like an overgrown Snap-Tite model. While there have been a few, somewhat more ambitious proposals—such as boosting the shuttle's fuel tanks into orbit and refitting them—none of them have ever been adopted. Nor has anyone ever added rotating sections to the real space stations.

The harsh reality is that working in space proved far more difficult, dangerous and time-consuming than anyone had imagined. Even these simple assembly jobs sometimes require hours of effort.

Nor did Ley's vision of space planes ferrying back and forth from orbit regularly prove to be realistic. While NASA originally announced an ambitious schedule for the new shuttle, which assumed that an orbiter could be refitted, refurbished and ready to launch again in a matter of weeks, it was quickly forgotten. Once again, reality was far harsher than anyone had realized.

Which is more than a little reminiscent of what happened in 1929 when film auteur Fritz Lang brought in one of the top rocket experts in the world, Hermann Oberth (who would later be one of the key members of Hitler's missile program) as his scientific advisor for *Frau im Mond*—a job which also included the construction of a rocket as a publicity stunt. While Lang's cinematic rocket ended up mostly accurate, (except for a curious decision to immerse the rocket in water for takeoff!) Oberth never finished the real rocket. He may have known more about rockets than anyone else in the world, but he still didn't have any idea how to actually *build* one.

Ley's spiritual heir was an American professor, Gerard K. O'Neill, whose book, *The High Frontier* offered an even wilder vision of man in space. While Ley's space stations were filled with astronauts, scientists and explorers, O'Neill envisioned us sending up thousands of average people to live in space. He pictured lunar mining operations shooting raw material out into Earth orbit, with vastly lower energy costs than launching from Earth. There it would be turned into vast orbiting habitats, monstrous cylinders or spheres, with bands of farmlands and waterways—and, of course, zero-gravity sex hotels at the poles.

His habitats have shown up in almost as many places as Ley's creations: perhaps the most familiar is *Babylon 5* (although the show rarely ventured into the wide-open main habit areas of the station).

However, they would require incredible amounts of spacewalking labor to construct, even if the materials arrived at L5 in some easily assembled form. With our space program currently in disarray, they look even more unlikely than Chesley Bonestell's elegant wheels.

And one has a sneaking suspicion that Larry Niven got it right in *The Patchwork Girl* when he portrayed low gravity sex as awkward and technically challenging rather than blissful.

There have even been moments when out-and-out pseudoscience in science fiction has its origins in claims made by real scientists.

Take the curious case of psionics. Mental powers keep showing up in science fiction, even in the work of authors like Arthur C. Clarke whose visions of the universe were otherwise materialistic. Most of the blame for this seems to rest with famed editor John W. Campbell, who pressured his authors into working "psionics" into their stories for *Astounding* (which alienated many of his writers). He coined the term, combining "psi" (extrasensory abilities) with electronics. He believed that science would ultimately allow us to harness these powers as effectively as we could control the flow of electricity in a circuit, and even championed a supposed psionic amplifier, the "Hieronymus device."

But Campbell's obsession still had its basis in the work of a real scientist. He'd discovered the work of Duke University's J. B. Rhine, the founder of parapsychology, in the 1930s and was impressed by Rhine's attempts to bring scientific rigor to the study of ESP. Even the Hieronymus device had its roots in the claims (albeit highly dubious ones) made by an electrical engineer, although Campbell exaggerated them almost beyond recognition.

We now know that there were serious methodological flaws in Rhine's work—and no one else has ever duplicated Rhine's modest successes.

This did not dissuade large numbers of people from believing him at the time. Or today, for that matter. Whatever one may think of his work, Rhine's greatest success was selling the idea of parapsychology to the general public.

It would be easy to dismiss much of the science fiction about nanotech as total fantasy. Books such as Neal Stephenson's *The Diamond Age* and Greg Bear's *Slant* paint dazzling portraits of worlds almost completely restructured by nanomachines: they steer flying machines without control surfaces; wars rage at the nanolevel; and almost anything can be made by nanofabrication methods. Others, like Michael Crichton's *Prey*, feature "grey goo," the monstrous runaway growth of self-replicating nanomachines. In Wil McCarthy's *Bloom* the goo has not only overrun Earth, but most of the inner planets of the solar system.

Yet, once again, much of this—including the grey goo itself—came not from their overheated minds but from the scientist who first popularized the concept.

While Richard Feynman first discussed the possibility of making such machines back in 1959, the concept burst out fully formed in 1987 with Eric Drexler's book, *The Engines of Creation*.

Drexler figured that man could do nature one better: instead of assembling his micromachines from unpromising materials that were little better than a soap bubble, Drexler conceived of nanoscale assemblers, capable of making his tiny machines atom by atom out of any material. He even coined the term "grey goo," envisioning it as one of the major hazards of his brave new nanoworld.

More than anything else, it was his images of microscopic machines made from single atoms, as if they were tiny tennis balls, that caught the public's eye.

Shortly after the book came out, Stanley Schmidt, the editor of *Analog*, encouraged his writers to read it, and then create stories using Drexler's ideas. Because these stories came out so soon after *The Engines of Creation*, science fiction has been the lens through which the public has viewed nanotech (and one of the reasons so many people fear it).

However, the scientific response was quite different: many challenged Drexler's more sensational claims. Dr. Richard Smalley—a leading researcher in the field, discoverer of the "buckyball," and an avowed "fan" of Drexler—has been among his most active critics and one of the first to offer an extensive critique of his claims. He found the nano assembler claims absurd and unworkable, noting scathingly in their 2003 open debate that "you cannot make precise chemistry occur as desired between two molecular objects with simple mechanical motion along a few degrees of freedom in the assembler-fixed frame of reference."

In fact, Drexler's machines face quite a number of unique challenges because of their scale: atoms are "sticky" at the quantum level, and reactions often require very precise amounts of energy at the right time and place. A nanosub trying to navigate our bloodstream would find surface tension, Brownian motion and the viscosity of fluids at that scale almost insuperable obstacles.

Instead, most nanotech research focuses on more achievable goals like fabrication methods and nanomaterials. Ironically, they now realize that softer, more pliable materials—like the lipids Drexler sneered at—

would do a far better job of handling the endless battering of Brownian motion. Rather than trying to outdo nature, they've found it easier to work "with the grain." As a result, current applications include devices built with DNA and RNA, and fabrication methods similar to protein folding. Rather than nanotech "boxes" that make anything we need, we will get pants that shed stains or even a combination shampoo and conditioner.

There has been one rather sad development, however, thanks primarily to the exaggerated public image of nanotech. Companies have made a lot of money on products with the word "nano" on the package, even though they may have little or nothing to do with nanotechnology. Some researchers have done almost the same thing, using the word in their grant applications because they know it increases the likelihood their work will be funded (and one has a sneaking suspicion DARPA is probably spending millions on dubious defenses against "grey goo.")

Some intriguing nanomachines are already in use, such as the triggers used for airbags, but for now at least, Drexler's most extreme claims seem unlikely, to say the least. Perhaps someday we will create the devices he imagined, even the fabled nanotech assembler. It just isn't going to happen any time soon.

Not too long ago, it was fashionable to picture scientific progress in purely deterministic terms. Our research programs would inevitably yield new discovery after new discovery, through an almost mechanical process of experimentation and observation based on the scientific method, until we unlocked every secret of the universe.

However, a close examination of the history of science reveals something completely different. The great scientific discoveries have all been made by thinkers who could look at the known facts and suddenly imagine some new way in which they all fit together. Einstein went from the dark night sky to a four-dimensional manifold that was finite and yet unbounded. Kepler suddenly saw how the new data he and Tycho had painstakingly assembled could still be fit into a heliocentric universe—if the planets did not have perfect circular orbits. Two young men playing with wire and plasticine models in the back of their classroom suddenly realized that the seemingly random pattern of DNA bases must carry the information they believed the molecule contained. A dream of a snake biting its own tail revealed the true shape of the benzene molecule. The list goes on.

Ultimately, the engine of science has always been human imagination and intuition. True, it often took years of painstaking work and rigorous experimentation to translate an insight into a workable theory—and a great many of these ultimately fail. But without these bursts of insight—even the ones that proved wrong—there is no scientific progress. We may not think of scientists as wild-eyed romantics, dreaming of fantastic futures, but sometimes they are. Sometimes they can imagine fantastic—if fanciful—futures in which their ideas get carried to the furthest limits, visions as wild as anything ever conceived by science fiction.

And that's not such a bad thing.

ABOUT THE AUTHOR

Mark Cole hates writing bios. Despite many efforts he has never written one he likes, perhaps because there are many other things he'd rather be writing. He writes from Warren, Pennsylvania, where he has managed to avoid writing about himself for both newspaper and magazine articles. His musings on Science Fiction have appeared in *Clarkesworld* and at *IROSF.com*, while his most recent story, "(Yet Another Episode of) The BIG Show" ran on *Cosmos Online*.

Consciousness as Story:
A Conversation with Ann Leckie

ALVARO ZINOS-AMARO

I wanted to start by asking you about your early experiences with short fiction. You leaned more towards the fantasy side of the spectrum (you had several stories in Beneath Ceaseless Skies, *for example). Can you talk a little bit about the shift in your focus from fantasy to science fiction?*

In fact, it has kind of gone back and forth. When I was starting as a writer I wrote two novels actually, that are in a drawer, and they're science fiction. They're both set in the same universe as *Ancillary Justice*. I decided that maybe I should focus on short fiction, and there were a bajillion reasons for it. There's no reason any novelist should feel like they *have* to do short fiction, but I decided I wanted to try, so I read a whole lot of it. I went to Clarion West, which also focuses on the short form. At the time I was only writing science fiction. I didn't have any fantasy ideas, and I didn't think of myself as a fantasy writer. But somehow I started writing fantasy stories anyway, and it turns out that editors, who weren't buying my science fiction stories, started buying my short fantasy. So I focused on fantasy, which is why almost all my short fiction is fantasy.

Did you consider becoming a fantasy novelist, as a natural outgrowth of your fantasy short fiction?

I did flirt with the idea, yes. In fact, I had at least one friend who thought I should. When I told her I was going to sit down and write a new novel, and that it was going to be science fiction, she said, "I'd love to read a fantasy novel by you written in your fantasy universe." But back when I wrote those two shelved novels I mentioned, I had already had the idea for *Ancillary Justice*—and honestly, I was afraid to write it. So for a while I ended up writing to the side of it instead. But the idea stayed with me for a long time, so when I decided to write the new novel, I knew I had to write *that* novel, and then see where I would go after that. That's why I went to science fiction instead of continuing with fantasy. But it felt odd; it felt strange because there was a different vibe to it.

Have you considered going back to fantasy now?

I have considered it. Of course, now nobody knows me as a fantasy writer! I probably won't write fantasy for the very next thing, but I might in the future. I like the universe I've built up, and it might be fun to approach it in a different way.

Going back again to an earlier part in your career, I wanted to talk a little about your editorial work on—Giga—Giga—

GigaNotoSaurus! [Gig-ah-no-toe-SORE-us!]

Yes, sorry, I was having trouble pronouncing it.

Actually, I could be mispronouncing it. It's one of those things you read but don't hear spoken. One day I was watching *Chased by Dinosaurs* or something similar, and the guy was calling it Jiga-notosaurus. I thought, "No, that's not the name of my magazine! It's giga-, not jiga. We don't say jiga-byte, after all."

Maybe he does. *Chased by Jiga-bytes*.

Exactly.

What drew you to work on the magazine? Were you there from its inception?

Yes. It was my project from the start. While I was concentrating on short fiction, I found that—probably unsurprisingly—I tended to write long. I trained myself to write shorter and shorter, just to learn how to do it. But a lot of my early stories were over ten thousand words. The number of venues that will accept submissions over ten thousand words long was minuscule. Even between seventy-five hundred and ten thousand, there weren't very many. If you were looking for the most places to send a story, you were best off below six thousand words.

But there are stories that naturally need to be a longer length. Beyond the selfish "Gee, I wish there were more places to send my stories," I thought it was fair to ask, "Who is publishing these longer stories?" That was the seed of the idea for opening up a magazine and filling that need. Which was followed by, "Yeah, right, like I'm going to start a new magazine."

A short time later, my mom died, and she left me a little bit of money. I considered what to do with it. I paid off some bills, but still had some left. So I decided to set some aside and start up, essentially, a token-paying magazine, one hundred dollars a story, and running only one story a month. I thought I would make it available on the web, and also as a downloadable Epub file, for people who don't like to read longer fiction on their computer screens and prefer their e-readers. So that's what I did, and I'm pleased with the results. I think it's been successful.

Considering it's just one story a month, you've certainly received great critical notice.

I had two Nebula nominations the first year *GigaNotoSaurus* ran. I was completely floored by that. The next year there was another Nebula nomination. That was a Ken Liu story. Of course, Ken Liu is highly visible and totally awesome, but it was astonishing nonetheless. After thinking about it, I also realized that the story lengths might be working in our favor. Where was the competition? The very reason I opened the magazine was that few places were publishing such long stories. These are online, easily accessed. So it became a little bit less surprising. But even so.

The magazine is currently still going, by the way. I've handed over editorial duties to Rashida Smith. She's been picking the stories and publishing them, while I'm formatting the ebooks and writing the checks.

Has this experience whetted your appetite for any other editorial projects—maybe anthology-related, or even possibly *Ancillary Justice* spinoffs?

The thought has crossed my mind. In *GigaNotoSaurus* it was just me reading slush, no assistants. The volume of submissions varied a lot. Sometimes it would be a dozen stories in a day, but it would ebb and flow, never predictable. I also read slush for *PodCastle* for a while, so I think I need a break from slush reading.

That said, there's something really fun about finding a story you love and putting it in front of other people. So at some point, when I'm not tired of slush reading any more, I'm sure I'll say, "Wouldn't it be fun to edit again?"

Do you find that your work as an editor for the magazine and podcast in any way informed or helped you hone your craft when it came time to write your novel?

Probably. One of the things that looking in the slush pile gives you is the kinds of things that the work of writers who aren't selling yet have in common. They're the same kind of not-quite-fully-developed ideas. Once you see a critical mass of that, it's easier to identify when you're doing it yourself. Which I think is why sometimes people recommend to try and get a slush-reading position, if you can, when you're starting out. Generally it's a good idea, as long you're not driven to madness by it.

I think I was saying this on a panel the other day. Nick Mamatas had a post about how oftentimes people are looking for slush reader positions, but there's rarely a chance to advance and do actual editing, or guest-edit a particular issue of a magazine, and that's really a shame. I agree, because half the fun is being able to say, "I picked this out, and you're going to love it." If you're only slushing you may not get to do that.

Regarding Ancillary Justice, *you've mentioned that the universe goes back a long time. What about the specific plot of the novel? Did you have that from the start as well?*

The basic outline is old, but the plot wasn't entirely planned out. The idea of ancillaries and multi-bodied characters is very old; the universe of *Ancillary Justice*, in fact, was built around the characters of Anaander Mianaai and Justice of Toren to a large extent. I'm not sure where the concept came from. I've been asked what made me think of multi-bodied characters, and I honestly have no idea. It just happened, and once it did, I constructed everything around it.

From initial concept to final finished product, it sounds like a lot of experiences went into the novel.

That's right; it has a really long history. From the time I first attempted a draft, it took about six years. But I had been pondering it for maybe another five years before that. So going on a decade. I'm glad that when I wrote that first novel, I didn't tackle the story I was afraid to write, because the world wasn't as well developed. I sent out that early version to a couple of places, and it didn't do anything. In retrospect, that was good—between then and now there's been a lot of development that I think has been good for the novel.

So as far as plotter vs. pantser . . .

Totally pantser. I was accruing and reshaping material for a long time. This is how I've been working on the sequels to *Ancillary Justice* as well. I usually know where I want to end up, and I know several landmarks along the way. If I don't know the landmarks, I panic, because I need to have those. The rest of my time is spent figuring out how I get from one landmark to another. I realize some people outline scene by scene, but I can't even imagine doing that.

Is Ancillary Justice *the first in an open-ended series of novels?*

There are three novels in this set, and no, I don't plan for it to be open-ended. Much as I love my main character—I would have to, considering how much time I've spent with her—I wouldn't want to be in a situation where I'm endlessly producing a series of books just about this one character.

No *Wheel of Justice* then?

[Laughs] As a reader, I actually love ongoing series. For example, C. J. Cherryh's *Foreigner* novels; I think she's working on book sixteen. As soon as each one comes out, I sit down and read it and I don't do anything else all day, because I love them. It's wonderful to go back to a world and to characters that I love. But as a writer, it would drive me bonkers! I want to do something different.

As you prepared to write *Ancillary Justice*, what kind of research did you do?

I did some research into AI, but discovered very quickly that it wasn't going to be helpful for me, because I was treating it as a conceit. What I discovered that was more useful was related to psychology and neurology. Some of that was very creepy and weird. One of the questions raised by a character that has a bunch of bodies is, "Who is a person to begin with?"

You might think that's a simple question, but it's not. I don't personally believe in the soul or something separate from your body. But if it's all your brain/body, what could possibly inhabit someone else's body? How would it work? I realized I was going to have to solve that problem for myself before I continued writing. It turns out—and this is where things get creepy—that particular sorts of brain damage can do really radical things to your identity and who you think you are. You can have brain damage, for example, that makes you think you're dead. There are people walking around who have suffered from head injuries or strokes that will tell you, "I'm dead." My grandfather, at one point, had a stroke and believed people around him had been replaced with people who looked just like them but weren't. He believed my grandmother was an impostor. That was in the back of my mind when I was thinking about my novel.

I also checked out Suzanne Segal's *Collision with the Infinite: A Life Beyond the Personal Self* from the library and read it. In it, Segal describes how she got on the bus one day and suddenly she felt her consciousness move out of her body. She spent two years hovering behind herself, and after that she became convinced she didn't exist, that she wasn't a person. Eventually she reconciled the state of lack of self with spiritual Buddhist ideas. Split-brain patients were also something I took an interest in.

They'll say into one side of the patient's brain, "Pick up something that matches this picture," and the hand will pick it up. But then when they ask the other side, "Why did you pick that up?" they don't know, but they'll make something up. That really made me wonder, how much of consciousness is you making up a story about the things that you're doing, but in reality it's a bunch of other systems doing them? There's no way to know that, and it's creepy to think about.

What was it that originally attracted you to space opera as the particular storytelling kit you wanted to use to tell your story?

I've been reading science fiction since I was really young, and space opera was always my favorite. Spaceships, battles, that kind of thing. When I was kid, Andre Norton was my favorite writer. There was a library not too far from my house and every Saturday I would walk down to it and get my Andre Norton fix. At one point I had maybe seventy-five percent of everything she had written—and that's a lot! I don't know if her work influenced my novel in a specific way that I can point to, but I can't believe that there isn't some Norton there.

You're currently writing the third volume in this series. What other projects are on the horizon?

I'd like to do more short fiction again. Even though I feel I'm more natural at longer lengths, I really enjoyed writing short fiction a lot. It's also weird to be out of inventory, because when you're focusing on short stories, you always have multiple things out there at once. When I ran out of material while working on *Ancillary Justice* I started to panic. Then I told myself, "Of course I don't have anything else out right now. I'm just going to have to deal with that." I recently told someone I would send them a short story for an anthology; whether I finish it on time, and whether they accept it or not, we'll see. But it will be a science fiction story, and I'll almost certainly set it in the novels' universe. *Ancillary Sword*, the second novel, is coming out in October, and *Ancillary Mercy* will be the final book in this set. But I've worked long and hard on creating this universe, and I'm sure I'll come back to it one day.

ABOUT THE AUTHOR

Alvaro is the co-author, with Robert Silverberg, of *When the Blue Shift Comes*, which received a starred review from *Library Journal*. Alvaro's short fiction and poetry have appeared or are forthcoming in *Analog*, *Nature*, *Galaxy's*

Edge, Apex and other venues, and Alvaro was nominated for the 2013 Rhysling Award. Alvaro's reviews, critical essays and interviews have appeared in *The Los Angeles Review of Books, Strange Horizons, SF Signal, The New York Review of Science Fiction, Foundation,* and other markets. Alvaro currently edits the blog for *Locus.*

Another Word:
The Best of All Possible Worlds
ALETHEA KONTIS

"Of all the places I've seen, this is the fairest of them all."
—Regina, *Once Upon a Time*

My favorite required reading book in high school was assigned not in English class, but history. Mr. Stafford was a bit of a progressive history teacher (for South Carolina)—we lucky honor students watched *Amadeus* and *A Man for All Seasons*; we read *The Prince* and *Animal Farm* and *Candide*. I loved *Candide* for all the wrong reasons.

For those not in the know, Voltaire wrote *Candide* (or *L'Optimisme*) to illustrate his disdain for the philosophies of Gottfried Wilhelm Leibniz by the use of incredibly jaded sarcasm. It is the story of a disillusioned young man (Candide) and his misadventures with a mentor who believes that we live in "the best of all possible worlds." The book is hilarious and brilliant. I identified with Candide and I even had a best friend who was my own personal Pangloss. She saw her own little world through rose-colored glasses and she is the happiest and friendliest person I have ever known. Only, unlike Candide, I have made it my life's mission to be just like her.

Yes, I recognize that horrible things have happened, are happening, and will continue to happen in this world, but I don't have to give those horrible things control over my life. I believe that I will get out of my life what I put into it, so I make an effort to spread cheer and goodwill wherever I go.

There's a reason everyone calls me "Princess," and *it's not because I told them to.*

I happily admit to being a dreamer, but I am also a realist. I grew up in math and science—I know the odds, and the range of uncertainty. I can hypothesize various outcomes of a situation logically and rationally. I have the ability to predict a bad result and sometimes I'm right, or I'm pleasantly surprised. None of this means I can't stop hoping for a better future.

So when did it become *la mode* to be such a Voltaire about everything? Cynics rule the roost now. Everyone is so much smarter than everyone else, and they're happy to prove it at a moment's notice. Especially if you are SO DELUDED as to be optimistic about ANYTHING. Don't you know that real life SUCKS?

Boy, I wish I was kidding about any of that, but I've heard it all. Back when I worked for a big corporation I jokingly called it "joy discrimination," but it wasn't really a joke. I received an inordinate amount of micromanaging scrutiny because I enjoyed my job so much. Obviously, I was doing something wrong. I wasn't working hard/fast/long enough. Never mind that my clients all loved me and I was making their companies millions of dollars a year. I had directors, vice presidents . . . all the way up to the C-WTF-O attempting to make my life miserable so that I would fit in. Eventually they got their wish. After some pretty extreme measures on their part, I did what any sane, rational person would have done in a similarly abusive relationship: I walked away.

I was told by former colleagues that there was no longer any laughter or energy in the sea of cubicles where I used to work. What can I say? I'm an optimist. We take those things with us wherever we go. Any subsequent workplace happiness or lack thereof was no longer up to me.

Joy Discrimination is not limited to the corporate world. Take the entire dystopian literature movement, for example. Worlds thrown into dark chaos and main characters who don't live anywhere near happily ever after . . . if they live at all. But that's *realistic,* don't you know. LIFE SUCKS, ALETHEA. DEAL WITH IT ALREADY.

I recently made it through a *Bones* marathon rewatch on Netflix. Somewhere at the end of season five (2010), Bones says to Booth, "I envy your ability to substitute optimism for reality." I wanted to reach into the television and strangle whoever wrote that line. Temperance Brennan's character is hyperrational and as logical as a Vulcan. Semantics aside, the logic here doesn't fit. It's like saying "I envy your ability to substitute up for fish." The opposite of "optimism" is "pessimism." The opposite of "reality" is "fantasy."

This has become the zeitgeist; so much so, that it has been sincerely suggested that I see a therapist for my inability to accept that everything is just going to end up in the toilet. Am I not allowed to go to hell in a glitter handbasket? Is optimism really such a foreign concept that those of us who subscribe to it must be deemed as mentally handicapped in some way?

I may be a romantic, but I am also a realist. The two are not mutually exclusive. I *can* tell reality from fantasy. I'm beginning to worry that a growing number of the population can't or choose not to.

After a conference or convention, I'm always asked if I "had fun." I'm always baffled by this question as well. "Fun" is an incredibly subjective term. Take this past BEA (Book Expo America) for example. I was in attendance at the expo all three days, with events every single night, and stayed in the city for more events two days afterward. Travel was a small nightmare. I struggled with my publisher. Bookcon was a complete morass of chaos. A dear friend passed away. I was called to perform at the last minute, with very little warning. I was smack in the middle of a personal crisis that included moving one thousand miles across the country. Oh, and I signed about five hundred books and postcards while suffering from tendinitis in both arms, so I was in pretty incredible pain the whole time. And I lost my voice, which happens to me about once a decade.

This was the *reality* of my trip. But the question remains: Did I have fun?

That trip was not only fun, it was epic in its amazingness. I will never forget this year's BEA. It was a rousing success, and I'm so glad I did it. I'd do it again tomorrow, pain and heartbreak and everything else included. But I'm an optimist. I believe that I can do anything. I believe that strangers are just best friends I haven't met yet. I believe that I live in the best of all possible worlds, and I mean to experience that world to the fullest.

Would *you* have fun at BEA? The answer depends on not only the reality of the situation, but also what kind of person you are under extreme circumstances.

So what does this mean for our future? What happens if the young people of today continue to equate bleakness with reality? I fear the direction this prevalent pessimism is taking us. I can imagine how a world like that would look.

And I'll either be right, or I'll be pleasantly surprised. If you don't mind, I'm going to hope for the latter.

ABOUT THE AUTHOR ————————————————

New York Times bestselling author **Alethea Kontis** is a princess, a goddess, a force of nature, and a mess. She's known for screwing up the alphabet, scolding vampire hunters, turning garden gnomes into mad scientists, and making sense out of fairy tales.

Alethea is the co-author of Sherrilyn Kenyon's *Dark-Hunter Companion,* and penned the AlphaOops series of picture books. Her short fiction, essays, and poetry have appeared in a myriad of anthologies and magazines. She has done multiple collaborations with Eisner winning artist J.K. Lee, including The Wonderland Alphabet and Diary of a Mad Scientist Garden Gnome. Her debut YA fairy tale novel, *Enchanted,* won the Gelett Burgess Children's Book Award in 2012.

Born in Burlington, Vermont, Alethea now lives in Northern Virginia with her Fairy Godfamily. She makes the best baklava you've ever tasted and sleeps with a teddy bear named Charlie.

Editor's Desk:
Secret Project!
NEIL CLARKE

I've been working on a secret project. Time to tell.

Clarkesworld has always tried to cast a wide net in its search for stories. In recent years, thanks to the amazing efforts of Ken Liu and John Chu, we accomplished a long-desired goal of acquiring stories in translation. In April, I was presented with an opportunity to take our work in this area to the next level.

I am pleased to announce that *Clarkesworld* has entered into an agreement with Storycom International Culture Communication Co., Ltd. to feature a short story originally published in Chinese in every issue. Each month, an all-star team of professionals intricately familiar with Chinese short fiction will be recommending stories for this special feature and I'll select which ones get translated and published in each issue.

As it stands, our goal is to launch this new endeavor without giving up any of the existing fiction slots, including the extra story our Patreon supporters recently unlocked. To cover the additional cost of this content, we're going to need your support. Later this month, I intend to launch a Kickstarter campaign to cover the costs of the inaugural year: three stories in the first six months—our ramp-up period—and six stories in the following six months.

A project like this is perfect for Kickstarter. No one has tried to make translation a regular element of a genre magazine before and that's something I hope will be exciting to readers both domestic and international. My previous Kickstarter project—funding *Upgraded*, which goes on-sale later this month—was very educational and provided me with the experience and confidence I'll need to succeed with this campaign. I feel rather strongly that Kickstarter should only be used to launch new initiatives and projects, so during that first year, we'll be focused on increasing our subscriber base to continue the program indefinitely.

I'd love to hear your initial thoughts. Obviously I'm excited about this opportunity. I hope that you are, too.

ABOUT THE AUTHOR

Neil Clarke is the editor of *Clarkesworld Magazine,* owner of Wyrm Publishing and a current Hugo Award Nominee for Best Editor (short form). He currently lives in NJ with his wife and two children.

About the Artist
IAN McQUE

Ian McQue works in videogame development at Rockstar North as assistant art director and concept artist. He has been part of the teams behind the acclaimed Grand Theft Auto series, Manhunt, Bully, and more. His personal work has been published widely, from *Imagine FX* magazine to books from Design Studio Press. In conjunction with Industria Mechanika he also designs model kits.

WEBSITE

ianmcque.bigcartel.com